The Catastrophe of Rob and Lettie

by Ted Campbell

Copyrights © 2024

All rights reserved.

Dedication

I dedicate this novel to love. May we all find and dole out
our fair share.

Acknowledgment

A special thank you to my brother-from-another. Your unwavering support has always been my soul's inspiration.

About the Author

Ted Campbell is a native New Yorker from Westchester County. He is a Purchase College graduate with a Master's in Acting from the National Theatre Conservatory in Denver, Colorado.

Table of Contents

CHAPTER 1

THE AM GRIND

Hundreds of New Yorkers streamed out of the Broadway-Nassau subway station at the Fulton Street exit. They looked much like rats escaping a newly exposed hideout. Most of them rushed to make it to their desks, food stations, or department store area before their shifts began and the work day commenced. Many employees were already running late. Unforeseen subway troubles caused extra stress, making everyone more unruly than normal. Cloisters of commuters crush past one another to get a good spot on the Coffeebucks line in the lobby of One Liberty Plaza. They behave like schoolchildren on a lunch line.

The sixty-six-story black monstrosity at the corner of Liberty and Broadway housed several promising cosmetic technology offices, insurance companies, mortgage bankers, and an assortment of other cubicle office spaces.

It was June, Twenty nineteen. Summer. The streets of Manhattan's Financial District were in recovery from a brutal thunderstorm the night before. Scattered wrappers and cups from the local fast-food places around the area skipped

1

through the streets under cars and public buses and trucks speeding by.

Patrons stepped through pothole puddles of milky black water wearing colorful rain boots under dull-shaded overcoats and umbrellas, ready for the occasional downpour that was common in the bubble of Manhattan. Where the east and west rivers met. A balmy mist lingered over the street like an unwanted summer guest.

Many workers thought the area to have a weather system all its own.

The sun struggled to make an appearance through the relenting clouds.

Still, it was shaping up to be a promising day. Robert Hamilton thought as he took his last step from the subway tunnel in a triumphant pause to deep inhale.

Rob made a habit of lagging behind the crowd upon his exit from the 4 train. He didn't like to get caught up in the madness of his fellow commuters during the early rush hour of people traffic. For the last few months, Rob had been on cloud nine over the success of his team' at Chariot Mortgage Group. Rob managed the highest grossing division companywide with seventy million dollars in loan revenue. He managed the team for the last six months since his wife, Arlette got him the job. Already, he was making a tremendous impression on upper management. All his employees took a liking to him quickly. He was the new life at company gatherings. There was even talk of Rob spearheading the entire east coast region in the quarters ahead.

Rob smiled with pride at the thoughts of his sudden success. He stood outside the building in the designated smoking area in front of the tall window-paned lobby. He was a smoker before marrying and moving into the Brooklyn condo he shared with his new wife, Arlette. Now, he could only enjoy the contact high from the lingering second-hand smoke before stepping into the office space. The smoke odor mixed with the scent of his cologne energized him, and he knew it would cause wonder in Arlette's imaginative mind.

Rob stood a broad-shouldered six foot, with wavy blond hair he kept slick back against his head. He had striking blue eyes like diamonds. He was a dapper dresser, too. Always had the up on the office fashion trends. He believed in looking his best, always, without a hair out of place. On that summer day Rob wore a navy-blue Armani suit and a powder blue dress shirt with a tie that pulled both items together perfectly. He carried his beige leather carry bag with scattered papers inside and a book he always thought he'd read on the train but never got around to. The bag was a gift from his wife for winning the position she set him up for at Chariot.

Arlette also spearheads a team that isn't doing as well as Rob's. Before they hired him, Arlette's division was the top-earning team in the region. Her attitude towards the staff cost the company to lose some of its top-grossing account managers to better opportunities. Most of her employees were explicate as to the reason they exited Chariot. Others left during their lunch hour and never returned.

Arlette was no favorite amongst the staff. She didn't care to be, either. Her father was a real estate mogul who brought in tons of business to Chariot Mortgage Group. They would never risk losing him as a client. Upper management being humbled by Amos Silver's generous business contributions promised his daughter a management position straight out of college. They even allowed her to work on her master's degree in business management while she learned the ropes at the company. Some of the senior staff attended the graduation. At Amos' insistence and expense. Arlette was his one and only child. His precious princess that could never do wrong.

Arlette's beauty was rich onyx skin covering her toned body smooth as a black pearl. She wore her thick, long, jet-black hair in a trail down her back to her petite waist. Sometimes she would wear it in a snake-like braid that crept down her spine and slithered across her back when she walked. Without heels, she stood a tall five/ten like a fashion model. Arlette had grown into the mother she never knew as a child. Her mother ran off with a musician from Chicago when Arlette was just two and was never seen or heard from again.

Standing by a smoker on his second fag, Rob thought about his heavy hitters getting in the office before six o'clock, preparing that first cup of stale coffee from the break room, before logging in to work on the month-end accounts. They predicted the team would bring in another seventy million in revenue by the end of the quarter. Robert celebrated, yet again, as the leader of the star-earning mortgage crew. The 'Atta-boys' and smacks on the shoulder would come so frequently that he'd have to take a day off for whiplash-related injuries. He was confident David Mendes and Patrick Clark were already on the phone with brokers, pulling in new business while they settle any un-hashed refinance business that needed closing before they counted the final numbers for the quarter.

Yes. Rob thought. *It feels damn good to be on top.*

He inhaled deep again and in the wall of smoke passing his face there was the faint smell of lilies and daisies rising from the potted plants in the large planters outside the hooded tunnel-like square that made up the entrance to the industrial lobby. The sun's rays had finally beat the gray clouds, and a beam of light touched Rob's victorious, upturned face like a spotlight. He smiled into it. He exhaled and began walking towards the revolving doors when a young man half his age slammed into him, nearly knocking him down. The boy mumbled some obscenity Rob didn't understand, and the young man didn't bother to look back to apologize.

"Look out, Mr. Hamilton!" The familiar husky, rasping voice of the security guard beckoned as Robert switched back to where he was pushed from. It came from the smoking area, and Rob's eyes met the turned-up face of Melvin Rodrigues. A Cigarette perched between two fingers, his eyes looking up the side of the mighty building — a finger pointing at something in the sky.

A large pane of a glass window from the fifty-third floor came crashing to the ground, shattering in the space where Rob had been pushed.

The smokers, other commuters, and onlookers simultaneously cast their glares up the side of the black building to make sure the sky wasn't falling or doomsday hadn't finally come.

Rob caught his balance and looked forward at the young man who hit him and nearly ended his life before he could turn the corner of the building. His eyes fixed directly on the young man's ass peeking out the top of his jeans. Two bouncing black melons like enormous grapes dangling from a vine. Rob's white cock stirred under his blue slacks and boxer briefs. He covered himself from the emerging erection. The boy looked back with his sharp hazel eyes and shot Rob a mean stare before he hiked up his black jeans by the loops on either side of his hips. Then he was out of view. Rob turned to the revolving doors. He looked back at the shattered glass and the crowd forming around the shard remains.

That's when he saw Melvin teetering his way.

"Are you alright, Mr. Hamilton?" He asked.

"I'm fine. What the hell?"

"I'll have to call management. You get inside--"

"Did you see that guy?"

"What guy, Mr. Hamilton?"

Robert tried to shake the wicked thoughts forming in his mind. "Never mind. It doesn't matter now. Thank you--" For the life of him, he couldn't remember the security guard's name.

"Melvin, Sir." He said with a similar grin to the one on the face of the black boy that nearly killed him. Robert stepped back. "You go inside. I'll see to this and keep you posted. Are you sure you're not hurt?"

"Yes. I'm sure."

He turned back to the revolving entrance and went inside, covering his swelling genitals with the gift from his wife.

Fumbling with his ID card trying to keep his erection covered Rob dashed through the security gate into the elevator bank. A car was already full by the time he arrived at the entrance. The doors were closing, and Rob lift the bag from his swollen genital area interrupting its work. The woman at the front of the car gasped as a few other office girls giggled. A processor from Rob's team, Raymond Coleman, had a tray of Coffeebucks coffee cups in his raised hands and caught a full view of Rob's struggling erection. He pursed his lips, raised an eyebrow, tilted his head to one side, and said, "See you upstairs, Robert Hamilton."

The doors slammed shut just as Rob could cover himself up again. He whacked his swelling dick so hard that the erection finally settled in the nest and was barely visible. He pushed the call button for the next elevator. The double doors to his right opened to an empty car. He rushed inside and frantically pressed the button to the thirty-third floor. The doors closed before anyone else could enter. Rob backed into the faux wood-plated elevator wall and signed in relief.

What was that all about, body? He asked himself but really, he knew the answer.

eaning there against the back wall of the elevator, Rob relaxed into the flight of the box gliding through the building, saluting each floor with an annoying dinging sound. He thought about the boy who crashed into him outside the office building. He was a young black man. Perhaps in his late twenties. Maybe a fast food worker or grocery store clerk or delivery boy with mocha brown skin and big muscles. Rob's growing attraction toward men started in college with his bisexual roommate that was into exploration and drugs. But Rob never confirmed that he was bi or gay. He was exploring. College was all about experiments.

A smirk opened his face as he glared at the news monitor on the front panel of the elevator wall. There was a quick article about the music artist formerly known as Prince, reporting his death and there being no will. Rob didn't understand all the fuss over another drug-addicted rock star's death. Arlette screamed at him for his lack of empathy for the superstar's legacy. She made a big argument about it all last night. By the end of her rant on how everyone should praise him like he were the modern-day Jesus, she was drenched in tears and out of breath like she'd just seen the rock star live, in concert - front row. All he could do was put his arms around her pulling her close enough into him that they were both shaking. Eventually, she quieted and they listened to the 'Purple Rain' album together. He thought it strange that 'Purple Rain' was the only CD of Prince and The Revolution she owned, being a devoted fan with such an enormous reaction to his passing and all. She wasn't even able to name some of his other more popular hits that even Rob knew. And he hated The Artist formerly known as.

Their four years of marriage had become a farce. Rob dread coming home to Arlette at night. It was easier to cross paths in the long walkways of the office where they could shyly wave in passing as if they hadn't shared a bed the night before. There was enough room in the office to create distance between them. The bed only supplied a narrow space of freedom neither would invade. There wasn't much talking without argument the nights he made it home before Arlette was asleep. Rob normally had an excuse to work late. Instead of coming straight home, he'd frequent the bars in the area around the job. Then one night, Rob finally decided to venture uptown to Greenwich Village to the historical Stonewall. The only Gay bar he was slightly familiar with. This was his first attempt to quell the rising curiosity that had been haunting him since college.

As he stood in the elevator with his back against the wall, Rob was the same timid man in The Stonewall nightclub. Terrified that someone he knew would catch him gawking at the muscled men with their tight shirts and jeans. Their bulging genitals call out to him like sirens at sea. When he was finally approached by a very handsome, tall black man and asked why he didn't have a drink, Rob shot out of the exit of Stonewall, leaving the tall black man unanswered and his own feelings unresolved.

Chapter 2
MID-DAY MAYHEM

The elevator slowed and then stopped on the thirty-third floor. Rob pushed his back off the fake wood panel wall to step out of the car into the elevator bank to the entrance of Chariot Mortgage Group.

The double doors of an elevator across the bank opened and Rob's rival, Richard Myers, stepped out and stood still as his eyes locked with Rob's. Richard had trained Rob. The two men never developed a friendship and Rich seemed to resent Robert for catching on to the tricks of the trade so quickly and flawlessly. There came a point in training where Rob reminded Rich of proper procedures and company policy. Richard quickly developed a resentment toward him then. The two remained cordial over time, even when Rob's numbers began to rise and Richard's began to decline. Without a word of warning, they were swift rivals.

"Robert!" Richard said, with a fake smile a little wider than the Hudson. "It's been quite a while since I've seen you. Are you gaining weight? You look a little pudgy around the midsection."

Richard was a gym rat who kept a strict workout that gave him Adonis results. He had a slim waist, a flat stomach, and a chest that looked like it was made of body armor. His arms were like the trunks of trees. Arlette would always compare her husband to Richard whenever she was annoyed with Robert. Richard and Arlette dated for a few months before she and Rob met and married. Often, to his face, Arlette would brag about Richard being a much better lover than Rob ever could be in bed.

"Good to see you, Rich," Rob said. "Let me get the door for you."

"No. That's alright. I think I got off on the wrong floor. I figured I'd stop and say hello since we haven't seen one another. How have you been? According to the numbers you're flying high on cloud nine."

"I hadn't noticed. The team works hard. We get results. We don't follow the numbers."

"Management seems to think you're the crème de la crème of the West Coast – with Colorado doing so well this year. I suppose that green gold has the whole country trying to cash in. I was promised that region before you came along."

"I heard that," Rob said. He held up his key card in a farewell gesture to Richard and tried to exit the conversation before much else was said.

"You stole those accounts from me." Richard's voice was flat and slightly threatening. Rob pulled back his key card from the wall sensor and turned to Richard looking prepared for battle.

"The region was assigned to me because management saw the hard work I put in for this company and the many others I've worked for. They thought I would be the best fit for the goals they wanted to achieve in the states my division handles. The proof is in the results, Rich. There's no mistaking that." He gave a slight smile to his nemesis. He could see in Richard's construed face that he hit a nerve using his rival's short name to address him. Arlette once told Rob that Richard hated being called anything other than Richard. Nicknames really got under his skin. Rob made a conscious effort to reserve 'Dick' against any further escalation. "Besides, wasn't it you who told me that you'd have nothing to do with 'Pot loans'? Isn't that what you called them: 'Pot Loans'?"

"I said that after they handed them off to your team."

"Because you thought they wouldn't pull in the number, right Rich?" Rob asked. "Well, your loss. If you'll excuse me, I'm late getting in."

"The bosses went with you as a caution. If everything didn't pan out, they would have blamed you and given you the boot without question'. You were the scapegoat. You just got lucky, Robert."

"Very lucky! If I might say so myself, Dick." Rob said with a victorious grin. "Good talking to you. Have a great day." Rob was already through the glass doors of the entrance, strutting down the walkway between the cubicles in front of his office before Richard quell the surprise on his face. Robert didn't bother to look back to see that Richard's face was beet red and it looked like smoke was about to billow from both ears.

"Robert Hamilton." An overtly official voice spoke up behind him as he passed the first line of cubicles closest to the entrance. When he turned around he found Ray Coleman standing up at his cube. He took a few sips from his coffee cup while Rob turned. Ray's dark brow over his smart brown eyes wrinkled into a questioning gaze.

"What is it, Ray?"

"I'd like a word with you."

Rob took a few steps back to Ray's cubicle and saw through the glass window door that Richard had just entered another elevator. He watched his rival's every step until he disappeared into the car.

"What do you need help with, Ray?" He asked, stepping into the cube and looking down at the computer screen.

"Oh, I'm not the one in need of help," Ray announced. "You may need some help if you don't have a conversation with your wife." Robert slightly gagged at the mention of the word, 'wife'. Until that moment, he was under the impression his co-workers were unaware of his marriage to Arlette. The two had agreed that they would keep the relationship a secret at the workplace due to the company policy on interoffice romantic relations. They were stringently prohibited. What Chariot Mortgage Group didn't know couldn't hurt them. Could it? Especially if they never found out.

"What are you talking about?"

"Arlette. Your wife." Raymond said snidely. "She came by just before you arrived. She looked frantic that you weren't at your desk. I thought she'd make a scene."

"Could you keep your voice down?" Rob asked, looking around the area. No one seemed to notice or hear the conversation. Rob needed to be sure. "How did you know we were married?"

"If I didn't before, I'm for sure now. I saw the rock on her finger and the look of frustration all over her face when she glared into your fish bowl and found you not there. A crystal-clear indication. And you just confirmed my suspicions."

"Did she say anything to you?"

"About what?"

"Anything."

"I don't talk to Arlette. She has something against me, I think."

I know for sure she has something against you. Rob thought. She detests Gay men like finding a fly in her soup. As far as Arlette was concerned, they could line all the faggots up in a row around the world, then let the bigots take aim and shoot. She was convinced Ray Coleman was a closet case. Ray never confirmed to anyone in the office that he was Gay, but his flair and slight flamboyance raised conversation in the break room. He would be the first fag Arlette would put on that line around the world.

"I'm sure she doesn't feel that way at all." Rob lied. "If you're done with me I'd like to get to my office. I probably missed a million calls by now."

"Before you go -" Ray said. He had turned back to his computer and played with his mouse in a way that pricked Rob's ego. The only sound in the cube was the clicking of Ray's right index finger on the mouse. This went on without word for thirty seconds before Ray went on, "Raoul stopped by your office as well."

"What?" Rob said shocked at his own enthusiasm. Raoul was one of his account managers working out of Florida and occasionally visited the New York office to check on the crew. Raoul was also an out bisexual with a history of getting around with several staff members at Chariot whenever he was in town. Nothing concrete had been confirmed or denied but many rumors had surfaced about his conduct.

"That dude is Gay, right?" Ray asked in complete nonchalance as he kept his back to Rob. He fiddled with the mouse some more, making the cursor spin around the double screens with no real intention. This annoyed Rob even more. He knew Ray was making small talk – fishing for some juicy gossip. Ray was not one to keep secrets yet he knew everyone's private business. The women loved him.

"I wouldn't know about Raoul's private affairs. He's a co-worker."

"Really?" Ray stopped the cursor on the screen and looked over his shoulder at Rob. His black lips were curled in a grimmest as his eyes searched Rob head to toe. "You both seem so chummy whenever he's here. I would have sworn the two of you were much closer than co-workers."

"Are we done?"

"I suppose." Ray snapped back around in his seat and fiddled with the mouse. This time he opened a blank email page. "Now that you've got all your messages. Should I bill the company, or will you be handling this assistant service out of your own pocket?"

"Whatever, Ray," Rob says as he exits the cubicle. He nods in the direction of the new employee in the cube across from Ray. He'd forgotten the young man's name after hiring him just last week.

When he finally made it to his office, he closed the dark faux oak door to the glass-encased room, which felt exactly like a dried-up fish bowl. The outer walls on either side were made of glass. A window looking out into the city skyline on one side and another looking out into the bullpen of hard-working Americans under his command. It felt more like they were watching him.

Why was Ray so concerned about Arlette's ring? And who she was married to? Had the staff drawn up a betting pool to see who had married the stern black goddess of mortgages while he was riding up the elevator? He snatched at his ring finger with his right hand. He always remembered to leave the ring on the bedside table. Why did Arlette insist on wearing her ring during her commute? Just before she gets out of the car she promised to hide the ring under the seat. It's what they agreed on to keep the marriage a secret.

The company had a strict policy prohibiting office romance, but it was barely enforced. The office rumor mill ran rampant with stories about colleagues hooking up after company parties. A few office romances spawned a couple of children out of wedlock over the years. Rob and Arlette promised one another - and Amos Silver, her father - that their marriage would remain a secret until one of them got a job at another firm. Preferably Robert was Amos' take on the dilemma.

What was Arlette trying to prove with that damn ring on her finger?

There was a knock at the door and the phone rang simultaneously waking Rob from his daydream. He grabbed the receiver out of instinct and turned his head to see who was at the door before wedging the earpiece between his crunched shoulder and the left side of his head. He looked like a deformed Ken doll.

"Robert Hamilton's office." He said. He held up a finger to Marvin from Human Resources to wait. He forgot about their meeting this morning. Marvin pointed at his watch and held out his open palms.

"You finally at your desk, hot stuff?" A deep male voice crooned through the earpiece. Rob's cock stirred slightly. He shifted in his seat. "I stopped by to see you. We should talk." At first, he couldn't put a name to the soothing voice on the other end of the line. But it was familiar. The peppered Latin accent lacing the English he spoke brought focus on a devilishly handsome face in Robert's memory. Then a memory of seeing that same face staring back at him last night at a gay bar in Chelsea. Last night he'd shrugged it off and didn't see the face again. It was now that he remembered where he'd seen the man before.

"Raoul?" He whispered.

Marvin knocked at the door again and peered at Rob through the glass wall. His palms stretched out even further in frustration. Pointing at his watch, he signaled the time to Rob again. Rob covered the phone mouthpiece and mouthed "reschedule" to Marvin, then uncovered the piece again. Marvin shook his head in disbelief, closed the cracked door, and walked away.

For a moment Rob couldn't speak. He sat in his executive chair dumbfounded with the thought that he had been outed and his future with the company over, once the news got back to his wife that his office man crush found him in a Gay bar – when he should have done a late night at the office - Arlette would have his head. Worst of all, the secret he had been hiding since college would be exposed.

"What are you doing for lunch?"

"That was you at the nightclub last night."

"I said we should talk. When are you free?"

"I'm not free. I'm not like that." Rob had to contain his voice. He turned further from the glass wall facing the cubes. His brow quickly became sweat-damp.

"Robert Hamilton. Relax." An instant calm came over Rob as the warm sound of Raoul's exotic tone trickled through his eardrum. He heard every syllable as if for the first time. Raoul's accent spiced the sound of his name so Rob had to squash a sudden urge to dance salsa on his desktop. "Listen." Raoul sharply said. "I have no plans to tell anyone who I saw at Charlie's Bar last night. I know how to keep things private. There's an account I want to talk to you about. I thought I'd stop by for lunch."

Rob couldn't speak. He'd been so careful. He kept a low profile in his haunts, standing in the back against the wall of whatever bar he ventured; careful not to make eye contact with any man for too long. He'd harbor in the shadows, watching the other men dance, kiss, and grind on one another, having the time of their lives openly, in a place where it was perceived safe. Even for Rob to watch and imagine, was safe. He hadn't gone that far since college with his roommate. The urge had grown into a constant thorn poking at his backside. And the more he tried to make a good life with Arlette, the harder the prick poked at him. Life with Arlette was particularly unbearable last night with business calls and working after-hours at home, he needed some kind of release. That was how he ended up at Charlie's Bar last night. He told Arlette he was going for a walk and ended up in the Greenwich Village coming out of Midwood Brooklyn. He didn't get home till long after midnight. Arlette was knocked out, in front of the TV, on the broad sectional.

"Are you still with me?" Raoul said. Rob finally took a breath.

"We should talk. I want to talk to you. About this account." The phrases blurt from him like a confession. He turned to the window wall facing the cubicles and saw Ray Coleman standing up looking over his cube with the phone at his ear staring into Rob's dried fish bowl. Robert felt the urge to duck under the desk to ignore the glare. "I can't do lunch. Stop by my office at the end of the day."

"I can do that," Raoul answered. Then said, with a taunting smile in his voice, "Perhaps we could go out for a couple of drinks."

"I -"

"I'll see you at day's end, Robert." The line was empty before Rob could respond. He hung up before the dial tone sounded. When he turned back to the window, Raymond had gone from his cubicle and none of his other employees seemed to even notice he'd come into the office.

There was another knock at the door. Arlette's face popped into view through the slight crack in the entrance. Her eyes were shaped in saucer large circles that made the eyeballs seem to bulge from her face. Her dark sultry lips were pursed in a bleak frown until she saw Rob's spine straighten and the color leave his face. Her disapproving glare suddenly became a look of concern as she opened the door and stepped inside the office. She was careful to close the door fully and tuck herself behind it before she spoke to him.

"Robert, are you alright?" She asked. "You look like you're about to have a stroke." He couldn't speak her name, fearing whatever else might spill from his mouth.

"Robert," Arlette said Sternly. He didn't budge. Just a blank stare.

The true concern he saw in her eyes melted the freeze that had captured him. He felt a rush of blood push back to his cheeks and his forehead got hot.

"Arlette?" The true care in her brow settled him. Rob realized there was still love in her heart for him. Even if it was only a spark. "What are you doing here?"

"I work here. Remember?" The sass snapped right back into her words. That icy brown stare returned to its proper function. "I came to your office because I thought I'd ask you out on a date."

"What? Arlette this is a bad time to talk about personal affairs."

"Don't give me protocol shit, Robert. Are you in or out on a date night?"

"This is inappropriate behavior for the office. Why are you leaning on the door like that? You look suspicious."

"I don't look sexy to you?"

"Not in the office, Arlette?" Robert said. He snapped in his password on the keyboard and quickly opened his emails to be sure he hadn't missed another meeting. He shot a glance at the door and found Arlette slightly perched against it. Her sleeveless blouse showed off the perfect ebony of her skin blending with the dark in the faux oak wood. She was always the perfect arm candy regardless of her mood. A flawless black beauty with her father's disposition. "Have a seat, Arlette. Can we at least pretend we're doing business?"

"If you insist, Robert." She slid from the oak door like a python from a tree. Taking four casual steps to the seat in front of Rob's desk. She turned the chair so that it faced the computer. Her back to the glass wall dividing them from the bullpen. Arlette's river of black hair seemed to know exactly how to caress the back of the seat as it fell there. They both pretended to look at the computer screen as they continued talking.

"We agreed you'd leave the rock in the glove compartment before you came into the building. It was your idea."

"I woke up adventurous this morning." She said. "What do I care who knows?"

"The company?" Rob said with a shot of stern eye contact. He was clearly more concerned than she could ever be. "We could both get fired."

"Oh please. Do you think they would dare? The profit would drop the moment we walked out of here – with all of our clients."

"You're father's clients. These are your father's accounts. They're his friends."

"And we run those accounts and keep those client pockets damn full. I don't worry much about it. So, what do you say to a date night with me? I was thinking of Elmo. I know it's a Chelsea spot and you hate Chelsea, but I love being rude to the fudge-packing waiters. We had so much fun the last time we went there."

"That place is too loud."

"Okay. So, you're in?" Arlette said. She sat back satisfied and crossed a long dark leg over the other. "Where should we go instead?"

"I can't go on a date night tonight. I have a meeting with a manager about a few accounts." He wasn't lying. Not yet. "People are talking about your wedding ring."

"What people? What manager? Robert I'm trying to salvage whatever isn't happening in our marriage. We're not even talking about the elephant in the room."

Rob slowly removed his fingers from the keyboard and turned to Arlette. His brow raised in question. It was skimmed with a light sweat. "What elephant in which room, Arlette?"

Arlette's back straightened from the rear of the seat. She uncrossed her legs, keeping her knees tight together like the proper lady she was brought up to be. She stared into her husband. "Who's been talking, Robert? And what have you told them?"

"Ray said he saw you this morning when you came to my office." Rob Said. "Why didn't you just text or, better yet, wait till I got home? This is our place of business." He turned back to his computer determined to settle in finally. The consummate multi-tasker he'd come to be known for around the office.

Arlette seemed to deflate in her office chair. A shattered hope had doused the light luster she came into the room with, remembered and continuous. "I forgot to take it off this morning before I walked in. I was already in the elevator when I noticed it on my finger. Then I asked myself why? Why couldn't I wear it here? I'm proud of the decision I made. You've never worn yours? I should represent that choice." Rob wouldn't look at his wife. "That Ray Coleman is such a queenie busybody. He thinks he's hot shit." She looked out the window wall and saw Ray returning to his cubicle, coffee cup in hand. He caught her stare and tossed his hand in the air to flamboyantly wave at her. Arlette turned away without a response. "You should find some reason to fire that nosey queer. Why would I ever tell him anything about me?"

"You didn't," Rob said, still staring into the screen. "He saw your ring and guessed."

"And you confessed. You're a genius, Robert. Now the entire office is going to know all our personal business before days end. Did you tell him I was barren too?"

"Seriously, Arlette, not the place to have this discussion."

"Another elephant for another room, huh?" Arlette said in a raised voice. They both looked out into the work area and then quickly looked away.

The inside of the office graveyard was silent for a moment. The faint muffled sounds of the bullpen of cubicles rose in their silence. The crackling of keyboards, the muffled phone chatter, and rugged steps rising as the couple sat in silence staring into Rob's computer screen pretending to peruse a document. Pretending.

"Ditch your account manager and come out with me tonight, Robert," Arlette suggested. "You're right. We shouldn't do this here. And we won't do it at home -"

"I need to meet with Raoul about these new accounts. Tonight is definitely no good, Arlette. We'll make it happen another night – maybe month end." His voice stopped as he looked away from the computer screen to see quivering eyelids holding back two wells of tears. What was going on with her today? Any display of rich vulnerability was against her true nature. Why was this patch so rough for them both?

Arlette delicately dabbed the wells from her eyes as if something were caught in the lash. She smiled at her husband. The way she did in the silence when she asked him to marry her on the Brooklyn Promenade that chilly Sunday afternoon. It shocked her to hear him say yes. She swore he had no interest in her at all. She asked in hopes that he would shy away and leave her alone.

"Are we finished?" Rob said. "I should really get some work done today."

Arlette got up from the seat. Walking to the door, she said, "I'll be asleep when you finally decide to come home tonight. Don't bother to wake me." She exits the office with a small slamming of the oak door. It was enough sound to make the six employees in the cubicles in front of Rob's office look away from their work toward the gentle slam.

"Don't worry," Rob said under his breath. Once he was certain she had gone.

The hours that followed the day were much less interesting than the morning. Marvin from Human Resources came back to Rob's fish bowl to talk briefly about the paperwork that he was less than interested in completing. Rob nodded and shook his head at Marvin to keep himself from falling asleep at the drowning sound of Marvin's monotone chatter. He suddenly wondered about Marvin's marital status. Looking at Marvin's limp wrists at the edges of the arms of the chair, Rob didn't find a ring on his left ring finger. He wondered if Marvin were single. Gay even. He wasn't a handsome man at all. Balding with a scattered comb over with belligerent strands of hair that refused to lay flat. The thick bags under his eyes made them look like empty sockets. When he wasn't speaking his bottom lip somewhat hung open. But he was soft-spoken and seemed gentle. Rob liked that about him.

Through Marvin's droned speech, all Rob could focus on was the sound of Raoul's spicy Latin melody speaking his name through the phone line earlier that morning. The thought of meeting him later excited and frightened him. He wondered if Raoul would even ask him about last night at Charlie's bar. What would he tell him? What lie he would create? There was no way he could come out to his co-worker. And what would he confess: that he had a homosexual experience with a college roommate? He hadn't done anything since then accept go to the Gay bars. What if Raoul ...

Rob began to picture his co-worker's large masculine chest with light brown skin like a stick of butterscotch candy. He had gone to the gym with Raoul and seen him in the locker rooms nearly naked. Raoul had a body any man would admire. He seemed to be raised that way naturally. Thick muscles in every inch of his tall, broad, brown frame. Nothing too overt. He was a perfect size. Easy to see he had a marvelous body beneath his wears. Rob remembered getting caught by Raoul gawking at his body when he saw him leaving the showers and grabbing a towel. He confidently smiled at Robert then. As if to warn him not to play with fire. The memory worked through his thoughts and caused a stir in his pants. If he didn't get his thoughts in order he'd have to relieve himself. He squeezed his balls and hard cock between his thighs. He looked Marvin in the face for, what may have been, the first time since he entered Rob's office. Rob's erection instantly simmered.

"Okay, Marvin, I'm going to have to cut our meeting short. I'm expecting a call about some business in the Denver office."

"Remember what I talk to you about, Robert. The company promises to be very strict on these policies considering the losses incurred in last year's law suites."

"I'm well aware, Marvin. And we'll talk more about this at a later date."

"I expect to," Marvin said, as he headed out of the office.

Relieved to finally rid himself of his annoyance, Rob turned to the large window looking out over the east river and the Manhattan Bridge. The sun had finally won its battle with the clouds and ushered in a bright, welcoming afternoon. It was lunchtime and the cubicles were primarily empty with the exception of those workers that brought lunch and would eat at their desks. Rob wonder if those who did were as lonely as they looked. Stuffing sandwich halves in their mouths while clicking a document on the screen; working away their personal time.

He felt a sudden urge to urinate and realized he hadn't visited the bathroom since having two over-sweetened coffees from the break room that morning.

In the bathroom, he decided to take a stall and sit on the toilet instead of using the urinal. He hated the splashback. He wiped the toilet seat down before taking a seat to avoid further splattering from the commode water. Rob had a neurotic bathroom ritual he followed whenever using a public bathroom. If the latrine were especially filthy, by his standards, or bore a stench, he would exit without a second thought. The office bathrooms were always clean just before lunch when everyone was out. It was the rush of the afternoon that Rob wanted to avoid. Post lunchtime, the toilets went unflushed, the seats were littered with stray piss, and the stalls bore odors of various digested food trucks and fast-food places in and around the financial district. The combined scents were enough to make him want to vomit. Rob took late lunches or no lunch at all.

His bladder released the two cups of coffee and his body seemed to sigh with relief. As he urinated his cock began to harden slowly, as his thoughts lingered back to the image of Raoul at the gym after their workout months ago. He remembered looking down at Raoul's flaccid penis and thinking how big it must be when he was erect. He was suddenly more curious than ever to find out. The image of

Raoul's snide smile while catching Rob staring at him fixates on Rob's fantasy. He dreamed of Raoul standing over him in the gym locker room stroking his brown dick until it was hard as an onyx stone.

Rob began to stroke his cock, relishing the intensity of the memorized fantasy. Allowing his body to slump on the stool. He had a full erection in seconds. The quiet of the men's room made the fantasy louder in his thoughts. He listened to Raoul tease and taunt him while he played with his cock at a distance too far for Rob to reach. He couldn't get his own fantasized vision to turn entirely around to see the full glory of the man he desired. Instead, it taunts him in mean sexy glances with enticing slaps of hard flesh against a smooth brown, muscled thigh.

Then he pretends Raoul asks him: "Do you want it?" And Rob felt a burst of white warm fluid shoot from his hard loins like a bullet from a riffle. With a nearly inaudible exhale, his body released, Collapsing deep into the toilet seat. The spill of his bulbous, beet-red cockhead dripped into the toilet opening. Rob was spent.

Slowly he lowered his chin from the open air of the restroom. He opened his eyes to his reality and found a massive wad of jism splat against the inside of the stall door. It was beginning to drool.

"Oh, shit," Rob said, under his breath, as if he'd just realized where he's been. Pulling at the toilet paper roll to form a firm bundle of protection around his hand, he wipe down the mess. His pants were still down around his ankles and his cock dripped into his pants. "Shit." He noticed.

"Is that you, Rob?" Ray Coleman's voice echoed through the tiled room. Why hadn't he heard Ray come into the bathroom? All the stalls were empty when he came in. *How does he do it?* Rob thought.

"Coleman?" Rob coughed. "Hey there." Frantically pulling at the toilet paper, he desperately cleaned up the mess he made.

"Hey." Ray said elongating the 'e'. Rob could hear him at the urinal on the other side of his stall. How long had he been there? He wonders. What is up with this guy?

"Yeah. You had lunch at that Chinese spot across the street again, didn't you?" Ray demanded. Water slapping porcelain seemed to echo through the bathroom like a running faucet with no sign of closing. "I warned you about that place," Ray said. "Deadly."

"Yeah. So much for that advice." Rob let out a sigh and sat more comfortably on the stool. He thought it better to go with Ray's explanation for his outburst. It lent him more time to pull himself together and get Ray out of the bathroom.

The toilet roll dispenser cranked like an old porch screen every time he twisted off more paper to wipe down the mess. The smudge on the back of the door was clean but there was a filmy stain that had crusted over the spot. No matter what he tried Rob couldn't smudge the milky stain out.

"Is this an extended lunch for you, Ray?" He said, suddenly reminding himself who was the boss. "You've been away from your desk for over an hour. And this morning you were up and down in the break room. That coffee isn't free, you know. The company's got to pay for that."

"I'm sure that's one of the company's main concerns, Robert," Ray said. His flow had finally come to a stop. Rob could hear him zip his pants and buckle up. He was ashamed of himself for listening so closely. "I was with a client at lunch and there was an impromptu Human Resources meeting in the breakroom this morning. I didn't see you there. Didn't Marvin tell you about it? I thought you had a meeting with him this morning."

"Does anyone even listen to Marvin?"

"Well, you should have."

"Why is that?"

"Because the company has set down strict guidelines pertaining to its in-office romance policy."

"What?"

"It will not be tolerated," Ray said. Rob heard the water from the automatic sink burst from the faucet and saw the bottom of Ray's slacks and brown shoes beneath the stall door. The salty stain stared back at him like an unanswered important memo. "Should they find out employees are coupled up, they will be terminated."

"What the hell is that about?"

"There was an incident in another office. A woman was told her husband was having an affair with a guy at the office. I don't know much about it. I think it went down in the Atlanta office. But the company fired the employees and handed down this new policy as a precaution to the rest of us. Especially for people like you and you know who."

Rob felt sick to his stomach and thought he just might need to stay in the stall a bit longer to collect himself. Or un-collect. Or disconnect. He thought. His insides felt like they would fall out. He and Arlette were already in serious debt from their spending, the wedding, and the condo in Midwood, Brooklyn. They both had student loan debt. Her father would have to loan them money until they both found work elsewhere. Which would only add to the already heavy strain. Amos Silver was dead set against the marriage from the beginning. He always thought something was off about Rob and he made no bones about telling Rob to his face.

"You're doing alright in there, buddy?" Ray asked. Rob heard him pull hand towels from the dispenser and listened to them crinkle as Ray dried his hands.

"I'm good, Ray. Thanks for the update on the meeting. I should probably pay better attention to Marvin when he comes through."

"That would help. Good thing he called that impromptu meeting or else I wouldn't have been able to give you this heads-up, my brother." Ray said as he opened the door to exit. "See you back at the pull pen. Good luck with your lunch."

Rob heard the door close. It felt like he was finally alone again. He quietly got up from the commode, pulled his pants up, and put himself back together all the while staring down at the forensic evidence of his fantasy. If he had the time he would grab some wet paper and towels and try to clean it but what if he were caught? People would start to question and raise suspicion. And then what?

He opened the stall door and meticulously washed his hands. He rolled up his sleeves to clean his forearms of the filth he thought was there. All the while he tried to wash his mind clean of the filthy thoughts about Raoul. Without knowing how or why his affection for his co-worker had grown into a full-on desire that ached to be quenched.

Rob investigated the mirror at the stern white face of a man he had not seen since his promiscuity in college. This man had a lust for his sex. The same sex. That lust refused to be denied any further. There would be no more hiding in the back of the bar watching other boys play. Regardless of the sacrifice, the man staring back at him in that men's room mirror would finally get in on the game.

CHAPTER 3
LUNCH HOUR

It was lunchtime.

Down the block from the office on Liberty, Arlette sat in a quiet coffee shop sipping tea and eating the last bite of two spicy vegetable rolls. Since Rob wasn't going to show her a good time that night, she thought she'd splurge a little at the company's expense and have something solid for lunch. The usual coffee and whatever fruit she could find at the juicing vendors or corner markets on the way from a client meeting was the standard. Arlette was always at work on a deal that was going to break every record. She was racing against herself. Not long ago in her career, Arlette was the top producer in her region. The only problem was that the region – as a whole – wasn't doing well at all. Still sick from the mortgage crisis that caused a second recession and underwater from natural disasters that nearly wiped Florida off the map, there wasn't much business coming out of the southern region. Arlette's team struggled to hit their numbers every month.

In past quarters, she held the torch for the company higher than her husband was doing at present – before Robert was even her husband. Before she got him the job.

In private, Arlette banked on Rob failing miserably. She was more than confident he would fall flat on his pretty pale face. And she was even more surprised when Robert soared way above her numbers just months after getting hired.

Before taking lunch that afternoon, Arlette had a meeting with her boss. He wanted to discuss the falling numbers in her region and brainstorm a strategy as to how they should go about boosting morale amongst the employees. He felt the team wasn't pushing hard enough because their leader seemed preoccupied lately with personal matters; keeping the office door closed and making herself unavailable for crucial meetings with clients. Arlette stared blankly through him and heard nothing he was talking about. She didn't care about the decline in her numbers. She was more concerned with the decline in her sex life since secretly becoming Mrs. Robert Hamilton. A ceremony her father begged her not to go through with. Amos Silver told his daughter on the day she was to marry, that he would fly her out to Paris and let her stay until she forgot about that dirty white boy. If only she would call off the wretched ceremony that day. And he paid for the wedding.

"I'll turn this shit show into the biggest getaway bash those fucks have ever seen," Amos told his daughter with more panic in his eyes than Arlette had ever seen.

"How could you call my wedding day a shit show?" She remembers asking him as he walked down the long corridore leading to the church.

"I paid for it," he told her. "I can call the shit whatever I want."

But she would make nothing of his insistence. Back then she wasn't sure if it was love or spite. After four years of marriage to Robert, she was sure it was of spite over any love she thought she felt for her husband.

"Arlette?" Bill finally interrupted himself recognizing the glazed look that had fallen over her face. Her lips perched and her face set in a gaze that seemed like she was with him when she wasn't there. "Are you even listening to anything I'm telling you?"

She snapped from her trance like a keyword had set her free. She finally saw her boss and unapologetically said, "Not really, Bill. No."

"I could fire you, Arlette."

"But will you, Bill? That is the question. Will Bill be stupid enough to fire the woman who would take what little business we have out the door with her when she leaves?" Arlette asked. She sincerely wanted an answer. She was prepared to walk. There was no natural way of knowing if her brokers would follow, but they were loyal to her. Bill feared that loyalty more than morale. Arlette was daddy's little girl but once she got her foot in the door she made a name of her own. She wasn't about to let some white boy tell her what to do with her staff.

"Get out of my office," Bill said. His voice was even and calm. He turned from her and began to type out an email.

"What?" Arlette asked, leaning into his desk.

"You heard me. Get out." He sounded as if he were saying 'good morning' with a slight pleasantry in his tone.

"Bill, you're being dramatic -" He wouldn't look at her. The left side of his face was turning beet red. She couldn't see the right side but assumed it was all the same.

"Arlette, please leave." He said through clenched teeth.

Bill continued typing as if Arlette had already gone. When she finally did leave, she slammed the door so hard behind her, the workers outside his office peaked over their cubicles or looked up from their desks to see who the thunderous clap had come from.

Arlette Silver stomped through the aisle like a stalking panther. The look on her face cleared the path of anyone in the way. She pushed through the doors leading to the elevator bank, got in an elevator, and came straight to the café. She found a nice quiet corner by a bay window to fall apart in public.

She was never much of a crier. Arlette favored a more masochistic method of self-punishment. She would rehash old memories of the darker corners of her past whenever something upset her. It was even more vital when she had done something to cause herself or her family shame. She was daddy's little girl and only child that was given everything she asked for. However, her father was clear that she was required to earn it. And her stepmother, Ella Silver, would have it no other way.

The tea was still warm when she reached for the saucer and brought it to her lips to take a sip. The day was warmer and muggy due to the rainstorm the night before. The air is thick even in the air-conditioned café. Arlette sat by the window to feel the sun's heat as she sipped her hot beverage making the inside of her body toasty in a hot place. The heat reminded her of a day in the summer when she was a girl and her stepmother, Ella, left her in the sun for hours in the backyard as punishment for God only knows what. Ella was like that.

Ella set up a tea party for them to play together in the backyard that morning long ago. She let Arlette bring all her toys into the yard for the grand tea party. Then she served them all hot tea. It was Earl Grey. The blend Arlette was drinking now at the cafe. At the very peak of the day, the sun hung over the yard like a beacon and there was no shade to be found.

Then Ella disappeared.

The glare through the bay window of the café shined against the linoleum floor surrounding her in the heat of the light. It was a reminder of that day when she got so hot in the backyard that she beat on the locked back door for Ella to let her inside, where there was cool central air. She received no response. The child cried at that bare backdoor as the sun beat down on a hot summer day. Her stepmother stood on the inside of that back door while the child beat at it, pleading to get inside.

The child smacked and hollered until her little hands gave in and she fell out at the doorstep, weak from the beating. She looked up and in her faint state, she saw a white face in the black of the window. Ella. There she was. Little Lettie – as her daddy called her – was all she remember before the day turned black.

"Excuse me." Arlette snapped back as if waking from a dream. looking up she found a man that resembled what anyone would dream a black angel would be, standing at the other end of the table. She felt like she should cover herself to hide what feelings had spilled from her audible gasp. "I didn't mean to startle you. I'm so sorry." The satin-light sound of his voice was smoother than his clear brown skin. Arlette pulled her hands from the table and covered her wedding ring with her right hand.

"No." She said with her first smile of the day. "Just lost in thought." She was casual and still; unbothered. "What do you need? Money for a charity basketball team at some school." Her response came before she noticed the tea and scone in a brown napkin in his hands and realized the café had filled up. All accept the chair across the table from her. Then she looked down at her empty saucer and cup.

"Actually, I was looking for a place to sit and enjoy my snack before a meeting across the street." The handsome, tall, dark, muscular man said as he laid his snack on the table. "I'd go somewhere else but -"

"No. Please. Sit down. I should be leaving." Arlette said, getting up. "I'm only taking up space."

"Don't go. Please. Stay." The man said. He had wise brown eyes in a gentle face, fresh shaved for his interview, she supposed. Some instinct deep inside her wanted to kiss his soft brown lips. She nearly leaned in to do just that before catching herself. "It's not every day a man gets the opportunity to have a bite to eat with a beautiful professional at the other side of the table. Please, join me. I'll split my scone with you."

"I probably shouldn't -"

"But you should." There was a slight pause in the introduction. Then the two laughed shyly as their eyes locked. Arlette felt that she had known him before but not in this lifetime. And when they were familiar - back then - it was an intense rush of fire that fed through them.

She sat down again. The sun's glare through the window coats her back again, like a blanket.

"Would you like to switch seats?" The young man asked.

"No," Arlette said brightly. "I'm fine here. What is your name?"

"I'm sorry. It's Mitchell – Hendrix – no relation to Jimmy." That shy smile again.

"What?" Arlette looked at him questioning.

"Jimmy Hendrix the famous musician."

"Oh. Okay. I don't know of him." Arlette had heard the name, but she never listened to music growing up. She claimed it bored her. There were better things to think about than someone else's sorry, set to sounds. "I'm Arlette." She hesitated. Then, "Silver." The name fell out of her mouth as unnaturally as the day it ceased to be true. As if trying to reclaim herself in the introduction. Her left hand emerged from under the table. The ring finger missing the wedding ring she conveniently pulled off and dropped into her Luie bag. She offered Mitchell her hand.

He took it and after a brief, light shake, he nods and shyly smiles at her again. *I wish he'd stop doing that.* She thought. It had been such a long time since a black man had worked his way into Arlette's view. Her father taught her that black boys were no good, hustling thugs with no sense of direction. It didn't matter if they came from money or good stock. His generation was the last of the good black men and Amos wasn't blessed with a son.

He had a husband all lined up for his daughter. A young man Arlette had grown up with and their fathers were good friends. Arlette went along with it until she found, Harvey, cheating on her with a white girl from a public school. She found out later that he couldn't stand the thought of having black babies to raise. She never had the chance to tell him she was barren.

"Do you come here often?" Arlette asked as a finger tickled the rim of her tea cup.

"Only when I'm interviewing in the area."

"New job?"

"I hope so."

"What company?"

"Chariot Mortgage Group – right down the block. I've been trying to get in there for some time now."

"I heard about them. Strong lenders."

"You know the industry?"

"Very well."

"What do you do?"

"I'm a manager at the bank you've been trying to get an interview with."

"You're kidding?" Mitchell's face lit up like a candle. The reaction delighted Arlette almost to laughter. She looked away to hide her shy smile. "You'd think I'd met a celebrity. I apologize, Arlette. It's just that I believe meeting you like this might be a sign."

"Don't tell me you believe in that sort of stuff."

"In a way ... I do." He said. Again, that shy smile. "I believe in karma. What goes around comes right back around. That's why I try to put out more good than bad energy in the world around me. This way the bad energy has farther to reach before it can touch me."

"Sounds like a solid enough theory, Mitchell." She said, hiding her sarcasm behind a fake expression of raised brow and wide eyes.

"I know it sounds crazy, but it works the same way with the good too," Mitchell explained. Arlette admired his conviction. She continued to listen. "The better you do for the world around you, the better it will give back."

"Are you from the south?"

"Is it that obvious?"

"It's actually ... endearing." She didn't feel like herself. She wasn't. She had become the girl she once was. Arlette Silver. The softer version of the woman Mrs. Robert J. Hamilton is. Without the ring to hold her down in a wife's position, Arlette could be anyone other than her true self.

The couple jeered at something funny one of them said that made the two topple over with laughter. Hysterical, stifled bursts of giggles infectious enough to put a smile on some of the faces staring back at them – some in reverence. Others with pride.

Arlette's memories of the hot day in the backyard faded like whispers taunting the back walls in her head. She enjoyed the moment with Mitchell across from her, flirting with - what her father would call – disaster. It was nice to feel wanted and beautiful like she did before she even started dating Robert. She regrets working so hard to get his attention at the workfair the day they met. She regrets showing his resume to her bosses, getting him the job - his promotion.

"Do you know that white dude standing behind you outside?" Mitchell asked. It wasn't until then that Arlette noticed a shadow had fallen over the sun's light like a barren cloud. It rose behind her like an evil gray mist coming off a calm black river.

"Who's your interview with?"

"I... Uh... I think the guy's name is Hamilton." Mitchell said. "Yo. White dude is seriously looking down at you like he knows you, Lettie."

"What did you call me?"

"Lettie. Wouldn't that be your nickname? Should you have one?" *Damn, that shy smile again.*

"My dad called me Lettie growing up," Arlette said. She felt the sun on her back again, hard and heavy. "He was the only one until..."

The bell to the quaint café jingled as the door let in one patron and let out another. Neither of them noticed the ring. Both seemed caught up in the sunbeam's glow burning through the window.

"Arlette." She heard Rob's voice, faint in tone but stern in texture. It broke the trance. She looked up from the table and found her husband towering over them like a sheriff. "What are you doing?" He shot a glance of disdain at Mitchell, then back at Arlette. He said, "Who the fuck is this?"

She sat back in the petite wooden chair and delicately crossed her arms. She looked Robert deep in his eye, waiting for him to breathe before she said a word. "Well?" He sighed.

"I think he might be your three PM, Robert," Arlette said.

"That's it! Robert Hamilton." There goes that candlelight look again. Arlette chuckles. "That's who I'm supposed to -" Mitchell looked from Arlette to Robert and realized then what karma had stumbled him into. He had no idea how he was going to get out of it.

"Mitchell Hendrix," Arlette said as she collected her items and handbag getting up from the table. "Meet Robert Hamilton. I should be going."

"Where's your ring now, Arlette?" Robert yanked at her hand. "How do you two know one another?"

"OUCH!" Arlette's squeal was more shock than pain.

"Hey! Slow down, man." Mitchell was on his feet. There were gasps before the café went quiet. Arlette heard the cook and dishwasher talk more clearly with the tension in the dining room so thick.

"Thank you, Mitch. But that won't be necessary." Arlette was calm and didn't pull away from Rob. "Robert, unhand me." She said.

He did as she told him.

"You know better than that." She produced a business card from her purse and handed it to Mitchell. "Should things not go so well with Mr. Hamilton today, send me your resume. Perhaps we could work something out. It was wonderful meeting you today, Mitchell. Thanks for lunch."

"Wait a minute. My interview this afternoon was with a female candidate. The last name *is* Hendrix, but I don't remember a Mitchell."

"You probably read something wrong in the email," Arlette said.

"No," Mitchell said. "I was born female," he paused. "Not that it's any ones business," Mitchell said to Robert, who began to laugh in his face.

"What?" Arlette's voice was meek, just outside a whisper.

"Our meeting this afternoon is canceled," Rob said through his laughing, "I don't think we have any available positions for someone with your qualifications."

Arlette witnessed the good-natured smile that naturally graced Mitchell's face fade slowly into a look of understanding. Then pity. He showed not a hint of anger toward Robert. He had just witnessed the public breaking of a man and his wife. He looked embarrassed for Rob and couldn't stand to make the situation worse. He held out his hand to shake with Rob's. Robert refused the gesture.

"Well, it was a pleasure meeting you," Mitchell said, "I hope you'll keep my resume on file in case something should arise in the near future." Stepping past Robert, Mitchell casually walked to the door.

Arlette turned quickly from Mitchell to get to the exit before he could. She didn't bother to take a last look or show her embarrassment.

"Lettie." Mitchell said quiet enough for her to hear before the door slammed behind her.

The bell rang again as he exited.

Before Rob could let loose a victory holler, he noticed the other patrons in the café trying not to listen in on the conversation. They would raise their heads inconspicuously, but he knew they heard every word about his failed marriage. Publicly exposed now.

Rob did not turn around. He stood in the center of the tables and chairs amongst the other patrons stealing side-eye glances at him. He was afraid to move. He hoped that he would somehow vanish into thin air or suddenly have the power to make himself invisible.

A burst of female laughter shot out from a table behind him. He turned around sharply to find three women having various drinks and chatting. One of them looked up at him.

"What the hell are you looking at?" He said to her. She rolled her eyes and continued her conversation with her friends as another burst of laughter spilled from the table – bigger than the last.

With a vengeful huff Robert found the strength to leave the cafe.CHAPTER 5

Close of Business, Today!

For the remainder of the day, Rob seethed over a file he'd barely underwritten. He couldn't get his thoughts away from Arlette and Mitchell having lunch. Why did it matter that he was to interview the young man for a position with his team? He caught him in a cozy conversation with his wife. There was no way he could interview the man today. Let alone work with him.

And the way Arlette sat there smiling and laughing with him. I've never seen her that relaxed since we've been together. What's that boy got that I can't give her? Rob asked himself.

"And Mitchell isn't even a real dude," he said to the open documents on his computer screen.

Does she want your Attention? His other self asked.

The memory of Mitchell's deep brown skin melted into Rob's thought and encouraged a sensation in his groan again.

He's not a real guy.

He pushed the thought aside, hoping not to have another instance where he'd need to relieve himself in the facilities again. The images persist with intensity, though. he fought hard to resist. His imagination took hold and began to run wild with the vision of Mitchell's seemingly soft brown lips and the black finger-waved hair Rob imagined was neatly tucked tight under a dew rag at the end of the day. Mitchell was a well-put-together black man who resonated with black pride and true black masculinity. Traits, appealing graciously to Rob's libido. In the past, these traits caused Rob to follow such men into dark alleyways, gym locker rooms, and even public bathroom stalls in full recognition of his hunger. A look of encouragement and discretion to take part. Rob would follow, but he had never tried anything. When they made advances, he would run. But that fear was fading – melting in the awakened heat of an aroused desire for the same sex. Seeing his wife there at the café across the table from his desire made him jealous. Not of her admirer. No. Robert was jealous of his wife.

Mitchell's not really Mitchell, Robert. The voice in his head laughed as he laughed at Arlette in the cafe. He shook his head. He wiped his hand over his face.

His eyes wandered from the forms on his computer screen to the view outside his thirty-third-floor widow of upper Manhattan. It was fading into night. The workday was ending. The sun was setting over the East River, and the traffic on the Manhattan Bridge was growing heavy. The dismal thoughts of his catastrophic marriage lingered while he sat still in the office chair of his fishbowl success.

'*I love Arlette,--*' Rob would remind himself every morning when he woke up by her side. He reminded himself while he contemplated his desires at his desk. The desk that Arlette stuck her neck out for him to have a seat at when she recommended him for the job. *I love Arlette.* That mantra mulled over his mind like a school teacher grading final exams. The words began sounding more like a command than a gentle reminder to remain faithful. Had the last four years of his life been a complete lie?

He remembered the first day he saw her at the job fair in the Jacob Javits Center. He was flustered from a long commute out of Brooklyn. He was sleeping on a couch at a friend's place while looking for work. A folder full of resumes dropped to the floor of the Utica Avenue station as he transferred to the A train. Most of the forms were lost to the crack between the train and the platform. The rest were splayed on the subway car floor and stepped over by the other rushing commuters. He was only able to salvage four. And nine of the resumes stayed in the folder during the fall. The job fair was hosting over a hundred companies looking to hire.

I only need one. He thought optimistically on that faithful day. *Just one.*

It was the view of Arlette from behind that drew him to the Chariot Mortgage Group booth. Under her formal office attire, there was no mistaking the tone and supple textures carved into her figure. The swooping elegance of that long, precise, black braid that curved down her petite back was an enticement. If his resume wasn't sharp enough to earn him an interview, perhaps a little charm would get him a date for the night.

While making his way through the thickening crowd she turned to him and he nearly lost his breath. Her almond-shaped wide eyes beamed through a sea of smooth black skin. Her smile was like a clutch of pearls. Greeting the booth visitors with such powerful grace that it seemed like they were meeting African royalty. Right away Rob wondered if she were the CEO of the Chariot Mortgage Group banner so elegantly draped on the scaffolding above them.

The company booth was no less elegant. Its bold navy blue and white banner with gold lettering branded with the company logo and noble name. Pamphlets, flyers, and applications were neatly displayed on a long rectangular table covered in blue cloth with white trim around the edges. There were balloons in the same colors that formed a tower on either side of the booth. Rob thought it was a bit overdone for a job fair, but it was attractive, and the booth was crowded with applicants.

When Arlette saw him, she gave a faint smile and turned away with the greatest of nonchalance. As if she knew what he wanted when he looked at her and she wasn't going to buy into his game. Not at first glance, at least. Her stare told him she was open to a talk.

Rob couldn't resist the challenge.

"Excuse me, sir." Rob turned to the office door from the panoramic view of a suddenly foggy evening in lower Manhattan and found a small, old cleaning lady pointing at his trash can. "May I take your trash?" He snapped back from his reality. The cleaning lady's Spanish accent reminded him of his meeting with Raoul and he glanced down at the time on his computer screen. It was already seven o'clock.

"Oh my." He said. "Please, go ahead. I didn't realize the time."

"You are the last one here. The office is empty." The cleaning lady said with a smile. She entered the office quickly, trying to get through her duties unnoticed.

"I'm never here this late."

"I know. I never see you."

"I have a meeting." He didn't know why he felt the need to tell her this. The cleaning lady just smiled at him. She emptied what little trash was in Rob's bin into a larger garbage just outside the door. Rob watched her the whole time as she replaced the liner and put the trash back by the desk. She looked up at him again with a quizzical smile. There was a blanketed glare over his face like he had walked into a thick spider's web and hadn't noticed. He was looking right at the older Spanish cleaning lady but saw past her, into a past life. One where he had control over his desires for men. He could make love to any woman at will with great passion and satisfaction without a thought about another guy. But today. Today he let those urges get the better of him and worried how far he would let those urges go as the night progressed.

"You should go dancing." The cleaning lady said. The suggestion snapped Rob out of his dim thoughts.

"Why would you suggest that?"

"You need to loosen up. Too uptight. Take off your mask. When you dance, you are free. You can wear all the masks at once."

Rob wrinkled his face and stared at the old woman with a scowl. She only smiled back at him as if she gave him the most important advice of his lifetime. And as he swiftly pondered the thought of himself out of sync with the music on a dance floor in a Gay bar, he could feel a slight ping of that freedom she spoke about. He shooed her out of the office dismissively.

"Good night." She said as she left him all alone again.

Rob got up from his desk to step closer to the window. The day had given in to the night and there were graying clouds collecting in the night sky. The deep blue and the tiny icy stars were slowly covered by the cold gray. A storm seemed to be on its way back to the area. The threat was in the air. He contemplates going home to make up with Arlette. Stop at a corner market and pick up white carnations, her favorite flower. The simplicity of her.

Then he remembered Mitchell at the café and his cock stirred in his pants.

Mitchell's not even a real Mitchell, Rob!

"I know that," he said in a forceful whisper.

He reached his arms above his head trying to stretch the thought from his mind. He rubbed his eyes to get a better look at the city beneath him. The simmering street lights down below looked like the embers of a dying campfire that once blazed bright with productivity. The bridge was covered in people and cars fighting to make their way off the peninsula, back to family life or home alone to an empty apartment with memories of past lovers and dreams of future ones.

Rob felt left behind somehow. He had nowhere he wanted to be and no one he wanted to go home to.

Do your love, Arlette?

He was thankful for all she had done to make his success a possibility. But no matter how he made himself look the part he would never really fit the role. Keeping secrets from himself had helped him believe the lie of his life. While looking over the bleak city night, his reflection stared back at him. It looked him square in the face and smiled a sneer that was mischievous and haunting. Yet Robert did not feel the muscles in his face move into a smile at all.

He stepped back from the window.

"Hey there, handsome." In the reflection was Raoul standing at his office doorway. His forearms perched high on the doorframe showing off his huge biceps and pectorals. His long slim stout torso swayed into a narrow waist. He was wearing a white suit with a black shirt underneath a white jacket. His black tie was loose and dangling from his left hand. The top four buttons of his shirt were undone as the shirt struggled to hold down his broad chest. Rob's jaw dropped slightly. He collected himself before turning around. Raoul chuckled. "Caught you daydreaming, huh?" He said. "Was I in it?"

"Raoul! It's good to see you again. Please have a seat. I wondered when you were going to stop by. I was just about to leave."

"That's not true. Considering what you think I know. You would have waited here all night for me, buddy."

"I don't know what you're even talking about."

"Sorry I kept you waiting I got tied up at a meeting with some brokers at USI. You know those guys can talk your head off."

"It's fine," Rob said. He waved Raoul into his office out of the doorway. Raoul crept over to the seat in front of Rob's desk as if they were about to plot the perfect crime. "Should I shut the door?"

"We should be good. The cleaning lady said I was the last one here."

"This side of the office seems dead anyway." He crept back to the door and quietly closed it. "Better safe than sorry."

"Suit yourself," Rob said, trying to sound as casual as possible. He was afraid to look Rauol in the eye. He feared how his body would react. His fingers fluttered at the keyboard with no real intent. Raoul finally sat down in the chair opposite Rob's desk. He slouched a little in the seat and let his legs fall open. He began to rock his knees in and out as he chewed at the fingernail of his right thumb. Rob wasn't sure if Rauol was gazing out the window or at his own reflection.

"You said you wanted to talk accounts, right?"

"I did." Raoul sat up in the chair and squared off with Rob straightening his back. They both looked overly official as if they were mocking the idea of a formal meeting. For a moment they stared at each other quizzically from across the desk. Rob hoped Raoul could not smell the fear his pours emit.

"Is everything alright? Who's been complaining?" Rob asked.

"No," Manny said. "It's nothing like that. The pipeline is doing well and there have been no complaints. In fact, Robert, there has been nothing but kudos coming down the path for you, Mi Amigo. You've made an impression on the guys at headquarters and there's been talk about you, Roberto. Lots of good talks." The last flip of the r in his name made Rob's right leg quiver as it popped from Raoul's full lips. He had to crane his neck to keep from twitching all over.

"Glad it's all been good." Rob croaked.

"Most of it. Yes." Raoul teased.

The words steeled Rob like a prick in the side. His back straightened a bit more.

"But you know there's always gossip and the haters who hate your success. Now they can talk you down."

"So, what have you heard?"

"Does it really matter to you?" Manny said. "I mean, you're the company's highest-earning executive for two of the four quarters straight. What do you care what people are saying about you? Unfounded office chatter can't break what you've built, Roberto."

"I should hope not."

"Besides, I heard you're at your best when the hell hounds are at your feet. Even with all the smack they talk behind your back, your team pulls in the numbers. I thank you for it. It keeps my belly full, mi amigo." Raoul slapped a thick heavy hand against his flat stomach and rubbed the rocky mountainous surface of his black shirt two times. He sat back in the chair and started to swing his knees in and out again,

Rob watched the sly smirk on Rauol's face deepen. It served as an example of the mischievous thoughts lurking behind those soft brown eyes. There was a sudden urge rising in Rob to jump across the desk and ravage Rauol's supple tan lips with as many kisses as he could steal before getting pushed to the ground. But what if Rauol enjoyed the sensation and allowed the kisses to transpire? What then? He was a Gay man after all. Rob saw him last night at the bar.

He looked away from his desire at the papers sprawled out on his desk, trying to hide the urge, he'd convinced himself was so transparent. Raoul's legs rocked in and out keeping time to Rob's pounding heart. That's when Rob saw the bulge slowly forming between Manny's rocking legs. He nearly stalled his gaze to hungrily stare at the bulge but turned away again. Back to the workload.

"You seem teased, Robert," Raoul said. "Has the conversation got you nervous?"

"No," Rob said snappily. "I'd just like to get home. It's late and Arlette might start to wonder why -" He stopped himself too late to even realize what he spoke.

"Arlette?" Raoul asked. "You mean to tell me you're seeing the evil bitch that got you this job? What is she doing, forcing you to fake a relationship to save face?"

"She's my wife, Raoul," Rob said in fain defiance. "I actually married the evil bitch after she go me this job." It felt good to say the words even if the content was false. Regardless, he hated to see Arlette discredited by her colleagues. She was labeled 'the bitch' because she's a scrutinizing and savvy businesswoman, not because she was moody and unpredictable. She had one goal, and that goal was a plane ole success. Winning. Why should she be ridiculed for that?

"Married?" Raoul said, scrunching up his face. "You're kidding me, right?"

"I am not."

"But you're -" Rauol looked up at Rob before he could speak again. Rob wasn't sure how he'd react if Rauol actually said the word aloud. Then it would be a question to the greater public universe. Then it would be a question that beckoned an answer he was not ready to give a reply to.

"What am I, Raoul?" Rob asked him. He made a point to focus his sharp clear blue eyes on Raoul's brown ones. His back was straight to Manny's slouching. He looked like a high school principal reprimanding a belligerent senior.

"I saw you in that club last night," Raoul said. "I don't need an explanation but, I'm sure your wife would want to know what her husband was doing in a Gay bar, propped against the back wall, trying to look like he didn't belong there – when, clearly, you wanted to be there."

Rob deflated.

"Don't talk about my wife."

"What are you going to do, Robbie Boy?" Manny sat up in the chair opposite Rob's desk. His back is erect and his legs are spread. His manhood now bulged against his left thigh like a thick piece of driftwood in a cavernous creek. Rob slouched a little in his seat and folded his hands on the desktop. "Huh –? Tell me some lie that you were with an old college buddy that turned Gay. He was too chicken shit to hit the bars on his own? Do I look stupid, Roberto?" Rob wanted to say yes; try to gain some sort of leverage in the confrontation. But his secret was out. What sense was there in hiding from it now? He lowered his eyes in defeat only to sneak another look between Raoul's legs. The bulging cock over his left thigh had grown slightly as a strong impression of the bulbous head formed at the tip of his stiffening rod. Rob's shoulders sank. His spine drooped to a slight sag. His jaw fell in a small gasp. Beads of sweat leaked from the top of his brow down his right cheek then drooled to a drip from his chin. He felt like he was melting in his seat.

"What's his name?"

"Huh?" Rob said, eager.

"Your Gay friend you were at the bar with last night. What's his name? Maybe I know him."

Rob had known Raoul D'Costa as long as he'd known Arlette. They were all at the Jacob Javits's Center Job Fair the day that began Rob's career with Chariot Mortgage Group. Rauol was a non-believer in Roberts's talents at an interview. Arlette had to urge Rauol to vouch for Rob when recommendations were called for. Arlette told Rob later - after he was hired, and they were married -Raoul felt: "You were hiding something". Their relationship as, Accounts Manager and Sale Representative had been strained in the beginning while Rob was still learning the nature of his new position. There were several times Rauol's temper was high, he'd hear the Dominican man's voice sound like a cross between a Latin singer and a Black Southern Baptist Minister. Rauol was a Latin son raised all along the southern coast and had the crazy accent to show for it. Rob could hear it coming out now and was surprised to hear it up close, in all its comic glory. It had always been an image in his head as he held the phone from his ear, to ease the pain of the preaching Bossa nova on the other line. Now there it was. In broad, beefing flesh. More a threat than ever before.

"You don't know him. He's very new to New York. I think it was his first time in the bar."

"Is that what you plan to tell your wife? I can't believe I'm even saying this! When your sneaking around in Boy Bars comes to the light, you're going to tell your wife that lie? That's the plan, Roberto? Seriously?" This seemed more upsetting to Rauol than it should be. Rob thought. He seemed personally offended by the notion that Rob would lie so easily to his wife about something so threatening and careless to their vows. Rob didn't understand how Rauol could care so deeply for a woman's situation and couldn't care less about the woman herself. A woman who despised men like him. Scorned men like Raoul. "I don't believe you," Raoul said. He leaned back in the chair again letting himself slouch a bit more and spread his legs wider. His torso was still straight as an arrow though, and he looked like a gladiator coming from a cocktail party after a wild pit fight. His thick thighs seemed to have grown muscle in the rocking. They seemed bigger now and the bulge had grown tighter. His legs rocked slowly in and out. Rob sunk his gaze into the desktop.

"You can look at me, Robert," Raoul said. "I remember the first time I started having desires for guys I was just sixteen and would strike a woody every time I was in the showers with the other guys after some sports practice or game. They wouldn't tease me about it because I was this size even back then. Just not as many muscles. But I could beat any one of their asses and fucked them after. If I wanted to. And they knew it. I was really into sports and played on every team I could make time for. It kept me out of trouble and off the streets where the bullies wouldn't take what little money my parents could give me, and I wouldn't end up on drugs.

My coach, Coach Lansing, was the football and baseball coach for my high school and he personally took time to train me, poaching me for colleges and a career in sports. He was a good-looking man too. Big white man with a barrel chest that swelled with muscles and I could always see the tiny dark hairs playing with the white cloth of his t-shirts. I'd get so horny during our sessions I'd need to push down my hard-on to keep it from showing."

"Why are you telling me this?" Rob was breathing heavily. His thighs clamped together to stop the swelling of his own grown. It only heightened the friction.

"Let me finish, Rob. There's a moral to my story, Papi. Let me tell it to you." Manny said. His voice was so mild it calmed Robert like a cool gulp of water on a hot summer's night. He looked away from Manny and out the window into the black night. The gray sky and the lights from the city look more like embers in a grill as the clouds and the fog act as billowing smoke in the winds. "One night he caught me after a game before I went to the showers and wanted to talk with me privately in a private office they called a cage. The coach said the area was used by the wrestling team and now it was an abandoned space. He didn't want the other teammates to hear what he had planned for me. He always pulled me aside after practice or a game. I didn't think it was a big deal. But I'd never been to the cage with him before.

We entered, and Coach didn't waste any time telling me what he wanted me to know. There was no place to sit down. Just the gym mats all over the floor and the mirrors on the front wall. He popped on a light that dangled from the center of the ceiling and illuminate the rest of the room just enough for me to see where I was.

'Don't be scared.' He told me. I don't know why he said that because I wasn't. I was only hoping that what I thought was happening really was happening."

"I don't want to hear any more of this shit talk, Raoul," Rob said. "I need to get home." He didn't move. Raoul went on.

"He told me that he sees me getting a hard-on while I watch him at practice. He told me that he wasn't some pansy faggot, but he knew what I wanted, and he wanted me to have it."

"Stop this," Rob said.

"He pulled down his pants and Rob, let me tell you, I'm not sure if I'm imagining this or my memory served me right, but Coach Lansing's dick had to have been about a foot and a half long and fat as the end of a bat. I drooped to my knees without fail and I don't think we left the cage for several hours after the game that night."

"I'm not listening to this."

"I was late getting home that night." Raoul laughed long and hard. He even slapped his knee and bounced up and down once in the seat. "I had to tell you that Rob because I see you as the coach saw me. Struggling with it. And I want to help you out, Robert. Like the coach did for me." Raoul said. Sobered from the laughter his cock had gone a little flaccid but still bulged, with obvious wanting.

Rob saw Manny through the reflection in the window. His reflection was floating above the foggy city night like a wet dream he'd had a million times before that night. His swaying legs were like a ship inviting vacation from the role he hated playing. And there he found the erection in the reflection bold, thick, and pulsating. He was sure if Raoul had released it from his pants or if this was his imagination. He tried to resist the urge to turn around and face his reality. His urges got the better of him.

"Let me help you out, Robert," Raoul whispered.

Before Rob could see him fully the lights on the floor went out leaving only a track of emergency lights along the walkways and the lights of any fish bowl still occupied. Manny gasped softly, sat up in his chair from his seductive pose, and looked around. Rob could see the tension rise in his face and had to soothe it. He got the upper hand. He rose from his desk walked to the other side and kneeled down in front of Rauol so that he was eye-to-eye with Rauol's crotch.

63

"The lights cut off around eight except the ones in our offices. Should I shut this one off?"

Raoul looked down at Rob solemnly and took his face into the palm of his hand, then he rubbed the top of Rob's head, messing his blond hair. "Nah, I want to see this," Raoul said.

CHAPTER 4
HOMEWARD BOUND REVELATIONS

Once she left the café Arlette had it in mind to return to her desk, look over a few accounts, make a few quick phone calls, then get out of the office early enough to beat any afternoon traffic heading back to Brooklyn. She'd make it to the Brooklyn condo by four and have the place all to herself the entire night until Robert showed up after she'd already showered and gone to bed. She could watch whatever program she wanted or some vulgar horror film that Robert would find atrocious. Then crank up the sound really loud, turn all the lights off in the house, and watch the scary movie in the dark by herself. Because he was too much of a pansy to watch the movie with her. That's how her father referred to Robert whenever he wasn't around. 'How's the pansy?' he'd tease Arlette during her visits with him and Ella, his white wife, at the house upstate where they raised Arlette together after Lettie's mom left her father.

The bustling lunchtime streets of lower Manhattan were proving to be more like an obstacle course than a slow walk back from lunch. The people traffic moved slower through the congested streets. She was a block away from the building and all she could see was a river of people to maneuver through in order to get to the front door. To the right of her was the road leading to the garage where she parked the Chevrolet Blazer for an astronomical monthly rate. She always had the thought to change the service to something cheaper, but the establishment was so conveniently wedged down a not-so-busy block and just steps away from the job, why should she cheat herself? What were a few extra dollars for safety and convenience? Penny's in the bucket. That's what. This was her quiet inner mantra since she learned the full saying when she was a ten-year-old girl. Penny's in the bucket. Fuck it.

When she arrived at the service entrance there was a Mercedes pulling out. The driver nearly ran Arlette over as he arrogantly beat at his horn and sped out of the garage with no care for the oncoming traffic.

"Asshole!" She shouted and flipped the driver the bird. The attendant came out to the curb to greet her.

"You alright, miss?"

"I'm fine. Here. Please make it quick I really need to get out of the city."

"Yeah. Don't we all." The young man said. He was walking away when she realized his handsome backside, with his square hips and muscled thighs in his fitted work slacks. It tickled her how many black men she had noticed in one day when so many days she hadn't looked twice. A tiny ping of regret danced around in her thoughts about how she was raised to despise her own kind. She wished she had disobeyed that command. Even with Robert's pansy persona, he was still a white boy. He didn't come from money. He paid his way through school. And was probably the highest-paid member of his immediate family. Robert wasn't the prince Amos Silver was expecting. But he was white. A white boy.

The attendant pulled out of the garage and got out of the car handing Arlette her keys. His smile was a string of white pearls perfectly set in his mouth like jewels in a crown. She wanted to kiss him as a tip. Instead, she smiled back.

"That's the first time you did that."

"Did what?" Arlette quickly raised her mask of defense by narrowing her eyes.

"You smiled back at me." The boy said. He couldn't have been older than twenty-five. His cheeks still wore baby fat and dimples. "I think I bring your car around every day and it seems like you have no idea I'm even here. It's nice to finally see a smile on your face. And you look up from that phone. It's a nice day after the storm last night. Isn't it?"

Arlette tossed her bag in the passenger's side seat and looked back at the grinning face of the attendant. It suddenly occurred to her that he was probably going to try hitting on her. Twice in one day was too much. "I bet the storm is on its way back." She said as she got in the car and slammed the door. She pulled out of the garage onto Washington leaving the attendant staring into the sky for signs of a storm.

Speeding into the traffic of the Brooklyn Queens Expressway, Arlette maneuvered her car into a center lane to flash through the traffic to the open freeway. A bright reflection of the sunlight burst through a cloud, smacking her windshield with a blaze of light that pushed her memory back to the day she blacked out in the heat of the summer in the backyard.

She remembered waking to her stepmother standing over her with the door wide open. The air conditioning turned up so high that the cool air was drifting over her like a winter breeze. She woke up to it. And her stepmother nudging her in the back with her foot.

"Get up, girl." She remembered Ella saying. "You could have died in all this heat."

Arlette pressed herself up with her hands and snapped her head back, looking at her stepmother like a viper ready to strike Ella.

"You get in here, Arlette," Ella demanded. "Cool off."

Arlette didn't say a word to her stepmother. Woozily she rose to her feet. Her favorite little white dress was soiled by the grass and torn from rubbing the concrete slab at the back of the house and beating on the backdoor. She shoved away what mess she could from it and pushed the black hair that had glued itself against her sweating forehead. She stared hard at Ella and didn't move.

"You get in here and cool off, Arlette."

Still refusing to respond she turned from Ella and walked back to the table and took her seat amongst her dolls at the plastic play set. She reached for her tea cup and saw she had just a bit left. She took the last sip. It was still warm and very sweet. She placed the cup on the table again. She looked at Ella standing in the doorway of the air-conditioned house. She could still feel traces of the cool air fading out of the open door. She remembered being thankful for it.

"Arlette, you get in here right now!" Ella shouted.

The little girl did not leave the backyard until her father was home and helped her bring all her toys inside while Ella watched. Arlette could tell that she was afraid the little girl would tell her father what her stepmother had done. But Lettie didn't say a word.

Not even later that summer when she got Lime's disease and was on bed rest for nearly two years. Her father asked how she got the disease the doctor said it usually came from ticks in the high grass. Her father started mowing the lawn more often. But that didn't stop the disease from stealing his daughter's fertility. Leaving her barren before she was a teen.

The little girl never said a word about what her stepmother had done.

An overpass blocked the sun's rays against the windshield long enough for Arlette to swerve to keep from rear-ending a car that had slowed suddenly in front of her. The quick maneuver nearly slammed her into another car to the right of her. The driver slammed on his horn and the cars barely missed one another. The driver threw Arlette the middle finger and screamed something she couldn't hear but could tell wasn't pleasant at all.

"The horn blows. Does the driver?" Arlette said to the empty cabin of her car. She was triumphant in handling the car without the aid of road rage to satisfy an intolerance for her fellow commuters. Making light of their anger was a better reaction to their hostility and it kept her out of trouble. Soon the whole congested scene was behind her and she was cruising down the BQE.Almost home at their Midwood penthouse.

The memory of that day in the backyard rolled around in her head like the raging sphere in a pinball machine. It bounced against the list of errands she needed to run, the clients she should call, and the husband she was losing touch with. All she could think about was the half-full bottle of whiskey she bought the night before. She was never a hard drinker until her relationship with Robert started to wane. Drinking was the only thing that would put her to sleep at night. To keep the thoughts of jumping off the balcony of their penthouse eight stories to splat on the sidewalk. To keep the ghosts of her childhood quiet, Arlette found Whiskey over ice. That was all she thought about as she parked the car in their spot in the underground garage, got out, and rush to the elevator.

She pressed the button, and the car came. It was empty. She got in and press the eighth floor. The door closed and didn't open again until it reached its destination. She fumbled in her purse for her key as she stepped out into an empty, low-lit hallway. Their apartment was at the far end to the left of the hall.

A feeling of dreadful anguish suddenly entered her from what seemed like frustration from her search for her key. Soon the tears flood her eyes and the dreadful feeling tore into her with such force that she threw the bag against the front door of the condo. Arlette smashed a hard-balled fist against the door that made an echoing bang through the empty hall. The sound seemed to ricochet down the hall and back again, knocking Arlette down at her threshold like a puppet with cut strings. She cried there for what seemed like an hour but could very well have been just minutes. The ugly past and her retched present had met her at the front door with a package of memories that was more than unpleasant; they were crippling.

Arlette's body heaved in huge sobs. At one point she even cried out maybe hoping that someone had been home in the other apartments and heard her and came out to talk or invite her into their home for coffee. Someone to ask if she was all right.

The hall remained empty during her rant. The elevator didn't even come to the floor. There were five other penthouses on the floor. One of the apartments was owned by an elderly couple that invited her and Robert over for homemade dessert last year sometime. The couple seemed to love Robert but acted as if Arlette wasn't even in the room at times during the visit. She didn't really know any of the other neighbors. She knew the couple at the other end of the hall were expecting. There was a hint of excitement on Robert's face when he told her at dinner that he spoke with the husband in the elevator one night and he told him about the wife being pregnant. Rob joked about how cute the kid would be with a mix of such a handsome couple. This made Arlette jealous enough of the wife that when she saw the woman, she shunned her before they were even introduced. Arlette refuses to speak to her as she watched her belly grow every month. They would accidentally pass one another on the way out of the building or take the trash to the incinerator. The woman would meekly smile at Arlette in an attempt to make contact, but Arlette would just look past her like she didn't want to see her and that growing belly.

If only that neighbor came out of her apartment now to see Arlette in the broken place she fell. There may have been a bond or the beginnings of a sisterhood. Instead, Arlette's cries were left heard by only her and the barren grey walls of the hallway.

She sobered from the break and collected the items that had been emptied from her purse. At the bottom of the handbag, she found the single key to the apartment and wondered how it had loosened from the ring. She got to her feet with the support of the door and the gray wall to the right of her. With a trembling hand, she forced the key into the lock and let herself inside. The door slammed behind her with a thud like the entrance of a tomb.

Arlette's birth mother left her and her father when she was only two years old. Marleen was a jazz singer before she married Amos Silver to officially become Arlette's mother. Amos promised that he would let her go back to singing after she gave him a couple of children and they were in school full-time. Once Arlette was born and the pressure of raising a newborn alone in a strange suburban white folks town – while her husband was away on business trips – became too much for Marleen. She had befriended Ella, just a neighbor then. She confided in Ella. Told her how bored she was, stuck in the house with nothing but a crying baby to talk at. She wanted her old life back. The wild music and lonely men take her dancing. Soon she told Ella that she was having an affair with an old drummer from a Jazz band she used to sing for. She told Ella about a plan she had to leave Amos for her lover. Marleen asked Ella to watch over her daughter until her daddy found another woman to care for them. Ella agreed. Marleen Silver left their home in Peekskill New York the night after she confide in Ella. Amos never saw or heard from his wife again.

As Arlette poured whiskey over ice in a small cube-shaped glass, she pondered what her life would have been like if she had known Marleen. If she had been raised by a Black woman. She wondered if she would have had a brother or sister or both if her mother had wanted to settle down, instead of whore around with musicians in the ratchet city. Why would she leave her daughter with a white woman who seemed to hate her and only wanted to take her place? Why? She pondered. Alone in the quiet kitchen of the lifeless penthouse.

She gulped down a hard swig of the chilled brown liquid, emptying the glass before coating the ice again. Looking disgusted with the bottle of Knob Creek she took a long harder swig straight from it. Enough for two shots. Head tilted way back. Her black braid dangled behind her like a snake from a tree branch. Her face folded inward when she swallowed and pulled the bottle from her mouth. She filled the cube glass before she put the bottle on the counter. The ice was swimming in the glass now. The clacking against the walls of the cub filled the room with a haunted rhythm as she walked to the bay window looking out over the L-shaped deck. They had a magnificent view over Midwood leading to the east side of Manhattan. No matter the night there was always a gorgeous view to stare at. A soft easy breeze flowed across the deck throughout the year. Even on the hottest days of summer.

Arlette grabbed her phone from the table by the patio door, a pack of Nat Sherman cigarettes, and a lighter from her bag. It had been their dining table. They both made a bad habit of making the table a drop-off stop for their personal items when they walked through the front door from long days in the office. They rarely ate together anymore. The table had become a jungle of personal drop-offs. Arlette went out onto the patio. The sun was setting behind the building leaving a little shine at the foot of the L-shaped terrace. She went straight to the shine and sat in the patio chair next to one of the baby trees Robert had decorated the deck with.

It looked more like a backyard in the sky than a deck on the roof of a Brooklyn high-rise. Various shrubs, foliage, and miniature trees lined the outer border of the terrace, alongside the earth-themed deck furnishings. Robert had taken great care to make the terrace an outdoor paradise. He was a wiz at gardening.

Finally settled in the deck, Arlette took another drink from her glass. She lit a cigarette and sucked hard from the butt. The smoke billowed from her nose and mouth like a fired-up locomotive. She felt her limbs give way to the ease of the alcohol coursing through her veins. It drowned out the voice nagging her about her white husband, Robert, and white stepmother Emma. She tried to focus on her birth mother and found no memory to lay anchor to. All she had to remember Marleen Silver were the sorted details of why she left. There were no photos of her. As a child, Little Lettie was too afraid to ask why there were no pictures of her birth mother anywhere. Majority of her life she had never questioned that Emma was not her biological mother. Then she started school and the kids would tease her because she was a jet-black girl with a white mama. And how did that happen?

When Arlette finally cornered her father – home from a business trip – he explained who Emma was to her and that her real mother had left them to run through the city streets with her man friends.

"She abandoned us, Lettie," he confessed to his young daughter then.

Arlette remembered seeing Ella at the door of her bedroom from the corner of her eye, listening in. *Nosy bitch.* She thought but said nothing. She remembered tears in her father's eyes as he tried to explain. She had no idea what the word abandoned even meant then. She only knew that her mother was gone and she wasn't coming back. But why would she leave me? Little Lettie pondered.

A tear rolled down her cheek to spill into the glass cub, mixing with the brown liquid that had thinned with the melted ice. She stared down at her phone between her legs on the cement-tiled floor. There was only one person who could absolve her curiosity. And he would be hard-pressed for information. She picked up the phone and went to the chain of text messages she had under the tag Daddy and opened the conversation. Amos was not the type of man to mince small talk with. He was a get-to-the-point type that didn't like to be disturbed. But his soft spot for his little girl was a surefire way to calm him.

Arlette knew that regardless of how her father felt for her if she posed her question the wrong way there would be no response at all. Finally, she wrote:

Hey Daddy. Hope you're well. I have a question about Mom.

The phone had barely touched the floor again before it vibrate indicating a response. She smiled and looked at the screen. It read:

Hey yourself, Lettie. Emma's just fine. What do you want to know?

Arlette quickly typed: *Not Emma. My mother. My real mother.*

The response didn't come back so quickly in that round of texting. The phone lay dormant with a black face staring back at her when she put it down on the floor again. She stared down at the phone for a while. Then took a drag from her cigarette. Then she took the last gulp of the watered-down whiskey in the cube. Finally, the phone brightened showing a new message. It said:

What do you need to talk about her for, Lettie? The woman abandoned us long ago. I can't tell you what I don't know.

Arlette furiously typed back:

What does she look like? There are no pictures of her anywhere. I have no idea what she looks like.

Look in the mirror: the message came in like he had read her mind. Then came another: *Especially now that you're a grown woman. You look just like she did when I met her. I always wondered if she made you by herself.*

The content of the message wasn't all that was surprising to Arlette. That was the first time her father spoke tenderly toward the woman that bore him a daughter he loved most furiously. She could even see the wonder in his eyes through the tone of the text message as he must have been when he wrote it out. The phone buzzed again in her hand. Another message:

But she left us alone when we needed her most and that makes her the ugliest woman to walk this earth. I try not to speak ill of her for your sake. But I see no reason to lie for her either. She went around with other men behind my back and she left you with a stranger.

That stranger became your new wife. Arlette was able to text back in between his speech.

Emma cares for you like you are her own flesh and blood.

She wanted to toss the phone into the bright blue abyss above her head when she read his message. If he had known the tortures Ella had put her through, he'd have eaten those words. He'd want her real mother back as much as she did now.

Emma only cares for Emma Silver, Daddy. She pressed the send button before she could second guess her hasty response. Amos was aware of his daughter's disdain for her stepmother. He was convinced it was a petty mother/daughter rivalry that would one day resolve itself. And when it didn't, he began to ignore it even existed. Pretending they made up in some imagined reality behind his back.

The phone lay there between her legs, black-faced and quiet. In the muddy distorted reflection of its face, she saw herself looking back at herself. Wavy and squiggled the design of the screen. The impression of her face was clear in the reflection. And for a moment she didn't recognize it. The woman there was familiar but slightly older and wiser in the face than the woman Arlette was. That woman was from another time. Then the phone went bright and a picture of a woman that looked like the spitting image of herself appeared on the phone. She had never seen the picture before, but the face was uncanny. It was her. The high cheekbones and broad black lips. And the long flowing black hair that fell around her shoulders was like the main of a lioness.

Arlette produced a gasp when she read the caption written by her father underneath the photograph. It said:

This is the only picture of your mother I wouldn't let Emma destroy. It was taken a year before I married her and two years before you were conceived. I kept it because it was the way I saw her before she was ruined. When she was a woman of the church. I loved your mother, Lettie. With everything I had. She didn't want the life I provided for her, so she ran away from it.

Arlette stared at the photograph through the phone and wondered how a face so familiar was so strange to her all the same. She traced the dark eyes and full lips with a fingertip and mouthed the word 'Mama' before her emotions could stop her throat. Some of the answers she sought were found where she knew she could find them. Amos had come through for his baby girl once again.

Then the phone rang in a call that looked to be from the office in downtown Manhattan. She swiped the face of the device to answer the incoming call. She put the phone to her ear. She got up from the patio chair and kicked over the glass before she could pick it up.

"Oh, Fuck!" She said unintentionally into the receiver. "Hello, this is Arlette."

"Good. I thought you wouldn't pick up."

"Tessa? Why are you calling me?"

"I know we have differences, Arlette but there is something I think I need to tell you." As Tessa talked Arlette went into the condo to get the hand broom and dust pan from the utility closet by the front door.

Tessa had trained Arlette in the position she resided in for the last five years. She applied for the management position but was beaten out by Arlette. Tessa was told she didn't get the position because she only had an Associate degree in Administration. Arlette had a Master's degree in Business Administration. The two women shared a brief friendship while they trained together. Tessa was never resentful of Arlette. It was her responsibility to get her new manager up to speed on a job she had been the substitute for six months before training her replacement. It was time to pass the office chair to the rightful head. Tessa had no problem doing that.

"I don't even know how to say this ..." Tessa said.

Arlette was back on the terrace bent over the broken glass, sweeping the shards into the pan. The inconvenience of trying to balance the phone between her raised shoulder and her ear while dusting up the glass caused the agitation in her voice. "You just say it, Tessa. That's how you start."

And that was the problem Tessa had with Arlette Silver, now Mrs. Robert Hamilton. No matter how kind a person you were to her the more cutting she could be. But if Arlette needed something from you she was the sweetest bar of chocolate on the counter. As soon as she got what she came for, it was business as usual. Let the slaying begin. Whip cracked!

"Remember when I told you I was interested in the security guard at the job and you told me to be careful of on-the-job romance?"

The question stopped Arlette's duties and she stood up from the mess, leaving the dustpan full of broken glass on the patio floor. She was sure she hadn't said anything to anyone about her marriage to Robert. So what if someone saw the ring. People talk. Office gossip is just that. Office gossip. She did remember the conversation with Tessa though. She tried to cloak her shame in a stern voice. She deflects by saying, "I remember our talk. What's wrong, did someone find out you're screwing the help?"

"Wow. I'm only trying to look out for you. Woman to woman."

"Oh please, spare me the jive, TT. Get to the point. What is this even about? I have work to do." Arlette bent down again for the full dustpan but missed the handle and tipped the shards of glass back onto the cement tiles. Some of the larger pieces broke into smaller ones and scattered further away. The phone slipped from its place between her ear and shoulder forcing Arlette to lose her balance trying to catch it. She fell to the tile floor as she heard Tessa tell her, "I know you and Robert Hamilton are married." In a desperate fit, she scrambled for the phone. It was in the middle of the spilled shards that looked like the inside of a shark's mouth. She reached into the center and grabbed the phone. As she pulled her hand away, it seemed like one of the pieces leaped up and bit her in the wrist. She snatched back her hand almost dropping the phone again.

"Arlette?" She heard Tessa's voice in her bloodied hand. The wound was already oozing blood and the shard of glass dangled in the pooling blood. She took the phone into her right hand and propped it on her right shoulder to speak.

"Arlette?"

"I'm here. I dropped the phone." She said. She sat on the deck floor to pull the shard out of her wrist. *I thought I was being careful.* She thought to herself. The strangest part of it was that she couldn't feel the pain of the cut on her wrist. It looked deep and there was a considerable amount of blood, but she couldn't feel anything at all. "Who told you I married Robert?" She confessed to Tessa willingly or not.

"That doesn't matter, Arlette," Tessa said. Her voice was grave and serious like a funeral. "My boyfriend Jose works in security in our building. We are watching your husband having sex with Raoul DeCosta from the Florida branch, in his office, right now."

"My husband WHAT! --" Arlette was trying to get up from the floor when her knee went down on a shard of glass that crinkled and crunched under the pressure of her thy. The glass cut into the dark skin of her knee and instantly produced crimson marks leaking from the black skin. Yet, she seemed not to feel any of it. She got to her feet as if she had been hollowed out or gutted. She suddenly felt like she was hanging from a hook and bleeding.

"Your husband is face down over his desk with a man thrusting him from behind—their pants around their ankles. The camera is not at the best angle, but I am sure that's Rob. I'm sorry if this is new to you. But I thought you should know."

Arlette seemed to dangle there at the patio door above the broken cube. Some of the shards were bloodied from her hand and knee. They looked like the teeth of a wild carnivore post-feeding. The last of the sun's rays had fallen behind a graying cloud. The sky darkened over Brooklyn but was darker over the Manhattan skyline. There, the view looked as if the sky was preparing an attack on sickness, with the force of a mighty storm. Arlette could feel that sickness rising in her as the blood let out of her knees and hand. The blood felt like it was replaced with a stormy rage. She watched her marriage come clean before her imagination.

The very accusation explained everything – even a personal curiosity she harbored since their wedding day.

CHAPTER 5
OPPORTUNITY KNOCKING

José Miguel was of average height and stocky build with tan skin and kinky soft hair. He was of mixed descent; his father was a black man from Alabama, and his mother, a native Puerto Rican raised in the Bronx, where she also raised Jose and his two sisters. He was the oldest and the man of the house after his father died on the job as a security guard for a bank during a string of heists in the late eighties. Jose had turned fifteen that year and promised himself that he would go into law enforcement when he grew up. The closest he had come to that dream was his job at One Liberty Plaza. A security guard for the insurance and mortgage companies on the upper floors of the building.

The pay was good, and the insurance package was top-notch. He had helped his mother put his sisters through college while sustaining his own place not far from where he had grown up in the Bronx. Jose took any shift anyone didn't want, along with his regular duty on overnights, where nothing happened except the occasional alarm going off because some idiot executive entered a fire door, or a cleaning staffer got stuck in one of the elevators. It surprised

Jose just how many people worked late hours in their office building, especially on odd days like Fridays or coming in over the weekend to go through files. They must have dying lives like the one he thought he had before he met Tessa. And Jose had been approached with an opportunity that would enhance his income by the thousands if only he were able to capture something good and juicy.

Friends of Jose had developed a website posting videos of funny content that people would upload for others to see. On the site, there was a more explicit area that was log-in protected and held more graphic video content. Some of these videos were voluntary and uploaded by the visitors. Others, videos from non-consenting sources performing indiscreet acts in places they shouldn't. Like the woman who was caught refilling the office milk container with her own milk. Straight from the breast. Or the Para-legal caught camping out in the office every night for six months before security caught him. The guy would have women sleep over in a tent he perched in the conference room every night. Jose was fascinated by some of the things his friends claimed to have posted.

"And they eat this shit up, man."

"They keep coming back like KFC, bro." His two friends were serious stoners from his college drop-out years. They majored in computer science and got into building games. They made a ton of money and decided to dabble in forums of their own for fun. Jose had a weed connect in college, though he didn't smoke weed himself, he'd make a profit off what he sold for his connect. He kept his clientele on a need-to-know basis. Pothead pals that could handle a habit and spent good money on quality. When he dropped out of school to help his youngest sister, Sabrina, with tuition, he held on to a few of their numbers to make a little money on the side. And he knew these two potheads would do great things with their clouded minds. Even if those things weren't for the greater good.

They told him about the site when he got the security job at One Liberty and made a proposition. If he ever could get some good footage of something ratchet or raw on the security footage at his office, he should send it over, and they'd pay him up to five grand, if the footage got any traction. Jose knew the offer alone was a violation of company policy. He would be fired, charges would be pressed against him. In fact, he'd not only get fired; he'd do time. He couldn't afford the life he was barely living at present. Credit cards exhausted, electric bill a month behind, student loan payments, he was lucky to make rent on time every month whenever he could. But if he did get some footage of something going down in a section of the building he was working, wouldn't that be priceless? How could I resist? Jose thought as he closed his locker in the basement of One Liberty. The security staff changed from their civilies to the duty uniform there. He was ready for his evening post on the thirty-third-floor security surveillance room, watching monitors for suspicious behavior that had never happened and would not need investigation for another night. If he was lucky, some cleaning lady would get stuck between floors in the stairwell.

"Yo, half-bread." The smoky rasp in the voice behind him he knew all too well as Melvin Rodrigues, a senior security guard. He was a nosey, creepy, fat guy who wore his hair in a comb-over and his uniforms way too tight. He had a bad habit of staring at people for too long. He was a smoker and hit on any female he caught out on a break in front of the building. Most of the women thought he was a stalker or some sort of weirdo. Jose didn't mind him so much. He turned around and found Melvin sanding at the end of the lockers with his shirt open, revealing his large gut under a triple-X white t-shirt. He was about to unbuckle his pants.

"Rodrigues!" Jose shouted. "What's good?" To his relief, Melvin took his hands away from his buckle to advance toward him. His face was contorted into a secretive grin with a plot brewing underneath it. Jose wasn't sure he'd like what Melvin was about to propose, yet couldn't help but listen anyway.

"You still got those friends that pay for sleazy videos?" Jose's eyes widened as he shushed Melvin with a finger to his lips. "What? No one is down here, half-bread. I might have something for you." Jose relaxed. He trusted the weird guy, but he was a little afraid of him, too. He only told Melvin about the proposition because he knew he was a nosey snoop. If Melvin had something, it would be worth at least a listen.

"This better be good," Jose said.

"He's here today."

"Who?"

"The fruitcake from Florida. The one I told you about. I caught him in the copy room with a staff member late one night at Chariot."

"Oh, the two guys?"

"Yes!"

"Oh, I don't want anything to do with that fag shit. Now, if it were two girls-"

"What are you talking about? You're paid if you catch them on the tapes."

"You're nuts, man. Why would I want to do something like that?"

"For the money, fool," Melvin said, getting in closer. "To expose those freaks for what they are. The sickness that they bring into our lives with their poisonous behavior. They should be burned for living in sin." Jose stepped back from Melvin. From the wild look on his face, he was scared the man was going to grab at him – or worse, beat him. "His kind are like animals. They like to show their sex. They know we're watching them. He's going to do it again and you should watch for it."

"I think you might want to see someone about your obsession, Mel," Jose said. He had nothing against gays. But he had nothing for them either. Clearly, Melvin had some sort of vendetta Jose wanted no part in. There was no way he'd catch the ass bandit on the security cameras anyway. He laughed inside at the idea. But he kept on a poker face for Melvin's benefit.

"He works with that chick you go with now. That Tessa – she's at Chariot too. She used to go on smoke breaks with that hot black woman. Arlette. I think her name is. I've smoked with her a few times. I think her husband's a fruitcake, too. I saw him checkin' out some black dude's ass this morning in front of the building. You heard about the accident this morning?"

"I heard something about it from reception."

"Yeah. It was him almost getting killed by the glass, looking at the boy walking by. If I hadn't shouted for him to move, the glass woulda killed him."

"He's Married to Arlette? How do you know that?"

"I saw her on a smoke break with the ring on her finger and asked when she got married. She told me all about her wedding. When she mentioned the guy's name, I didn't know he was the Rob who worked for the company till today, when I saved his ass."

Jose was running late to meet Tessa at his workstation. The mention of her name aroused him to end the conversation with his weird coworker and get to work himself. Catching up on office gossip was thrilling, but it wouldn't pay the bills.

"I got to go, Mel," Jose said. "My shift started."

"Look out for him, half-bread," Melvin said. "They want to be seen."

Jose shook his head and quizzically scrunched up his face as he turned away from Melvin to exit into the corridors leading to the main building.

He caught the service elevator up to the thirty third floor, where he stepped out into the secured hallway of the mortgage company. Chariot Mortgage shared the floor with the building security facility for the upper-level business spaces. Jose was looking down at his watch when he stepped out of the elevator into the quiet hall and made a left towards the security office. The time read nine fifteen and he was already late for his post. He hoped that Tessa had not been discouraged and left when he didn't show up on time. Halfway to the security door, he looked up from his watch and found his woman standing at the entrance to his station. She was dressed in a fitted white blouse that accentuated the curves in her breast. It had frills like flower peddles at the cuffs and collar. Her fitted work pants hugged her thick waist like a packaged ham. Tessa looked at him like a schoolgirl meeting the senior in some quiet place for their first time alone together. She giggled and smiled at him. The right side of his mouth arched.

"Hey, babe." He said.

CHAPTER 6
COLLEAGUES

Tessa Hernandez logged out of her computer at Chariot Mortgage Company at seven forty-five, minutes after her last associate closed out for the day and went home. Now that she was a manager of her own team – didn't matter how small – she liked to make herself available to every staff member. She thought it her personal responsibility to keep her door open for anyone to come in with an inquiry. And when she wasn't at her desk, she was on the floor or running a meeting in a conference room. Tessa had earned her Project Manager title without the benefit of a degree. She would make damn sure the CEOs of Chariot saw how qualified she was for the position.

Tessa came from a single-family home with five brothers and sisters. As the oldest, she had little opportunity to think about a future, much less pursue one. She got a job straight out of high school at a grocery store in the Bronx, where her mother raised the family out of a three-bedroom apartment along Mosholu Parkway. Tessa helped with the rent and school clothes for her siblings for three solid years before she got pregnant herself by the manager of the grocery store.

Her mother suggested that she quit the job and go on public assistance and help with the rent. When Tessa refused that suggestion, her mother put her out, claiming they didn't need an extra mouth to feed, especially if she'd have to babysit for free. Tessa packed up her belongings from the room she shared with her two younger sisters and left her family with just a suitcase and the shoes on her feet.

She found refuge with friends, sleeping on couches and spare rooms when parents of friends felt an overwhelming sense of sympathy for Tessa. Sometimes, she'd earn a week's stay, and one time, she was able to stay with a friend for a little over two months. The entire time, she held down her job at the grocery store without the manager knowing he had fathered a child until she started to show.

At six months, Tessa had gained a considerable amount of weight and there was no way of hiding the pregnancy any longer. She went to work on a Sunday afternoon after sleeping on another couch of another good friend's home and had been up all night with discomfort from the boy inside her kicking and keeping her awake. Her hair hadn't been kept since the pregnancy. It had grown wild atop her head. She had a permanently tired face that occurred when one gets deprived of sleep and carried a small human in the belly. That summer's heat kept her sweating in a way she wasn't used to. It caused a scowl on her face that turned heads in the opposite direction whenever someone saw her coming. Bitterly, Tessa took her cashier station and prepared for her work day when her manager - the father of her son – walked up to her booth to question her.

"What the hell is this?" He said, pointing at the belly that held his unborn son.

"My gut. What does it look like?" Tessa said. She investigated his round face and hoped her baby didn't arrive looking anything like his shameful father. His pudgy nose and full lips would be too much for a child's face. He was tall and lanky like a perched scarecrow. Tessa wondered what made the attraction to him so strong that she even wanted to have sex with him, on the job.

"I'm sure it's not mine." Tessa stopped breathing for what seemed like an entire minute. The words hit her like she had been pushed into a pool of cold water and was being held down at the top of her head.

A male customer pulled into her aisles behind her boss with a cart half full of groceries. He had a well-mannered child sitting in the front car of the cart.

"I haven't slept with anyone else, Bryant," Tessa said under her breath. "Who else could be the daddy?"

"I have no idea who you've been sleeping around with," Bryant said. "All I know is you slept with me the first night we went out. I knew you were an easy lay." Bryant made no effort to desecrate his words.

"Hey!" The patron behind Bryant said. "She doesn't need to hear that right now. You're a jerk. Get lost."

"I'm her manager."

"Which makes this situation even weirder." The man said. "Get away from her. Right now!" The child in the front car of the cart, who had his back to the scene, pleasantly turned to stare into Tessa's face. He was a tan child; he looked mixed race with his fiery red curls on top of his head and the sharp red freckles on his soft, bright tan skin. He looked like something out of ancient oil paintings. Then he smiled at her and pointed his tiny index finger at her belly and said:

"Baby." Tessa nearly broke down in tears at the register.

"Yes, Texas. She's having a baby -"

"Like mommy?" The little voice came again light and inquisitive. Tessa smiled at the boy and rubbed her belly with hope in her heart.

"Yes, nephew. Just like your mommy." The baby proudly smiled at his uncle, then shyly lowered his head, smiling.

"He's not your son?" Tessa said. "He looks just like you."

"His mother is my eldest sister." The man said, smiling at Tessa. "I have seven sisters. Texas is the ninth grandbaby."

"He's adorable," Tessa said.

"What? Are you flirting with customers now?" Bryant butted into the conversation. Obviously jealous. Tessa hoped he had gone away as he was told. Before she could defend herself, the customer snatched the opportunity to continue his heroics.

"You know, I've had enough of you, buddy. Step away from the register. Your employee has work to do." Bryant did not move. He was a considerable amount taller than the customer – Tessa had always been a sucker for tall, thick shoulder and stomach men. Bryant would probably beat the customer mushier than the cottage cheese she noticed in his cart. But the man had a spunk in his stark brown eyes that said he'd put up a hard fight. Finally, Bryant broke their gaze and turned to Tessa.

"This ain't over." He said before walking off. He looked back at them when he was half the distance away. Tessa's customer shot him the bird before Bryant could turn away, or his nephew, Texas, knew what was going on. Tessa and her customer laughed together. It had been so long since someone stood up for her.

"What's your name?" She asked with a grin. It came out flirtier than she would have liked.

"Oh no, honey." He said, waiving a raised index finger between them and pursing his lips. "I am Gay."

"I figured as much," Tessa said, as he unloaded his cart onto the conveyor and she began to scan the items. "Your nephew is really cute."

"Thank you." The little boy said.

"And smart!"

"Thank you, again." The boy said it in a witty yet shy dancing tone. They all laughed together.

"Is he the father?" The patron asked.

"Yes."

"You know you can get yourself a little lawsuit going if he keeps treating you like that."

"I don't know about all that."

"You should quit this place."

"Where would I go? I got to eat and pay rent. Where am I going?" Tessa pursed her lips, shook her head, and rolled her eyes.

"Take my card and call me in about a month." The customer fished a business card out of his wallet and handed it to Tessa. She read. It said: Raymond Coleman Account Management at Chariot Mortgage company.

"I don't know anything about banking."

"You're a cashier, Tessa," Raymond said. "You count money all day. Besides, you were smart enough to know that a mortgage company deals with banking. Most people are not as bright. Trust me." Raymond had bagged up his own items in a few recycled shopping bags he pulled from his satchel strapped across his chest. He handed Tess his credit card to pay the bill. She looked at the business card and credit card as if she had forgotten what to do. It was like Raymond Coleman was the fairy godfather she had always wondered when he'd arrive. He shook the card at her. Another customer strolled a cart full of groceries into Tessa's lane. She sighed and suddenly remembered her duties.

"You call me in a month, girl." She handed him back the credit card with his receipt and tucked the card in her back pocket.

"I will," Tessa said. "Bye, Texas."

"Bye, Bye. Tessa." The child said. She lay her palm on her stomach and Texas shouted, "See you later, little baby."

Later that month, Tessa was fired from the grocery store for showing up late. The final trimester had not been kind to her physically. She had developed a close bond with a co-worker named Gail who had an apartment and a couch she could crash on for however long it would take to get back on her feet after the baby was born. Tessa's first son was born in the middle of September in the same hospital where his mother was born. She named him Zachery. She stayed with Gail while she healed and looked for work. Zachery was already three months old when Tessa finally remembered the card and Raymond Coleman from Chariot Mortgage Group. A nagging whispered to her that Ray would remember that day in the grocery store. It also assured her that he would be able to help.

"Chariot Mortgage Group, Ray Coleman speaking," Ray said into the receiver, squishing it between his shoulder and the left side of his head. He was typing up an email at his desk when the call came through. "Tessa. Of course, I remember you. You had to have had that baby by now ... Zachery ... strong name. I like it. I'm glad you found my card. I have very good news for you."

There was an interview for a position as a mailroom attendant that paid double what she made at the grocery store. Ray got her an interview. When she got the job, he told her that this was just a stepping stone. That he would personally help her find her footing in the company and get her wherever she wanted to grow. Though Tessa didn't understand his generosity, she was thankful for it. She did all she could to live up to his recommendations. Soon she moved on from the mailroom to the processing floor, and within the year, Tessa earned a Mortgage Underwriter position. In five years, she was managing her own broker accounts. Her son was ten when the managerial position she currently sat in became available. It was Arlette Silver who recommended Tessa for the role. She pushed hard on her behalf.

Another good day. Tessa smiled to herself, pulling open the draw to her desk to fish out her briefcase and purse. There was a knock at the open door. It was Raymond. She sat up in the chair and smiled wider.

"Hey!" Tessa said.

"Look at you – all managerial and stuff," Ray said, standing in the center of the door frame. "How does it feel?"

"As good as it did three months ago when I took the position. And feeling so much better every day."

"I couldn't be more proud of you, T," Ray said. "We've come such a long way. Haven't we?"

"I wouldn't be here without you, Ray."

"How is Zachery?"

"Grown. He's graduating from junior high school this year."

"He's that old?"

"I know, right? When did we get that old?" They both sighed.

Ray stepped into the office and sat in the chair opposite Tessa's desk. They both looked exhausted from the long day of emails, broker meetings via Skype, and agents calling to complain. In each other's presence, they could instantly unwind and find a comfort that was unique to an at-work friendship. Through their experience, Ray and Tessa had created a bond like family. Ray had even put Tessa up in his two-bedroom apartment for a year after she was hired at Chariot. He helped her find a place and contributed to her moving expenses. Ray was named godfather to baby Zach, though there had been no formal ceremony. Whenever Tessa tried to repay him for his kindness, Ray would push her suggestions away. He made it clear that she was his sister in soul, and if the situation were the other way around, she would do the same for him. Tessa wasn't so sure about that, but she never let him believe otherwise. She was thankful for the support and never let Ray down whenever he called for her.

"I saw him today. He came by Rob's office."

"Who?" Tessa said. She was changing from her heels to her sneakers for her later commute home.

"Raoul. The Sales Rep from the Florida office. The one I told you about."

"What did you tell me about him?"

"That he cornered me in the copy room. He groped me. He tried to make me -"

"Ooooh!" Tessa said. Her head and torso shot up from below the desk like a marionette coming to life on a tiny stage. "I remember what you told me about him. Why didn't you go to human resources about that?"

"And look like the only fag trying to win a lawsuit? No, thank you, honey. I defend myself. I let it be known that was not about to happen. Especially not at the workplace. That security guard – the one that smokes with your home girl."

"Arlette?"

"Yeah. Her."

"We're not friends. She has no friends."

The conversation paused as the work history of Tessa and Arlette lingered between the two colleagues like an invisible mist of un-want never resolved.

"Well ... the security guy, Melvin. He came into the copy room when it happened and addressed Raoul. Raoul told Melvin he was horsing around. That security guard thought we were in on it together. He tried to reprimand me, too. Can you believe he accused me of being a party to that mess?"

"It's all coming clear to me now," Tessa said, rolling her eyes, and getting back to tying her left sneaker. "I remember how you railed about this."

"I should have pressed charges against that ass bandit for coming on to me. And that bigot that accused me of being in on that nonsense."

"What's up with Raoul? I mean, I've seen him. He's good-looking. Why would he need to force someone at work to do that?"

"No, girl. It was more about taking what he wanted and not being turned down." Ray said. Tessa read a slight fear on his face as Ray recounted the copy room incident in his mind. She could tell he was more afraid when it was happening. "The way he pushed me against that copy machine and reached for the front of my pants. I could already feel his big dick -"

"Okay," Tessa said with wide eyes. "Why are we even talking about this?"

"Because he's here again. And I think he's going after Robert J. Hamilton."

"Rob's not Gay."

Ray pursed his lips and narrowed his gaze on Tessa. "Maybe he doesn't know it yet."

"Ooh." Tessa chided. "Now you know you ain't even right!" They chortle loudly together, then suddenly stopped like the office was full of workers. "We're the last ones here – except Robert; acting like he's underwriting a file. When was the last time he did that?"

"What is it that you have against Robert?" Tessa mocked the way Ray repeated his name.

"He's a fake. A poser." Ray said. "Just because he has a physic and manner that help him pass in the straight community, that doesn't give him the right to fake an entire life at someone else's expense."

"Even if that someone else is a stark raving bitch?"

"Even if that someone else is a stark raving – what you said. I'm not going to call her that."

"Arlette was warned by everyone except that nasty stepmother of hers. There's something off about Rob. He's fine as mint China, but there is definitely a crack in the bowl. We just can't see."

"Well, that Ass Bandit seems to have seen that crack. He's been on the prowl since this morning. He had the audacity to come by my desk and ask, had I seen Robert? I ignored him. I didn't want to give security any more ideas." He sat back in the chair like a queen on her thrown post-affirmation of a beheading.

"I haven't seen her today. Not that I would have." Tessa said. She threw a miscellaneous item in her handbag and closed the bottom drawer of her desk. "I know she only gave me that recommendation because she didn't want to work with me when I refused to be the Maid of Honor at their wedding. I can't believe she thought we were friends or even close. She never liked me since she beat me out for her managerial position, and I was assigned to train her. Did I hold a grudge, then? No. I did not. And She thought that's why I refused to participate in the wedding."

"Why did you refuse?"

"I knew she was marrying Rob because she thought no one else would ever ask her hand in marriage. I knew that she thought no other man would want a woman who couldn't bear bear a child. I knew she was wrong, and I tried to tell her."

"She didn't want to hear you."

"She married him anyway."

"I heard he was drunk at the ceremony."

"While he said his 'I dos,'" Tessa confirmed. "Geneva in billing told me. She was one of the staff members Arlette's father invited to the secret ceremony."

"The two of them think nobody knows they're married," Ray said.

"Why would anyone care?"

"I know that's right," Ray said as he got to his feet and stood in front of Tessa's desk. He looked out the large window at the foggy night on the other side of the glass. A mist of white clouds passed by Tessa's window, making their reflections look as if they were floating in the white mist. "Looks like we're in for another storm."

"I hope it doesn't rain before I leave later with Jose."

"You're still seeing that dude?"

"I'm seeing him tonight, actually."

"While he's on duty."

"It's the night shift," Tessa said. "No one is here. He should have company."

"You should be ashamed of yourself. Why do you always fraternize with the help, T?" Ray was at the door.

"Goodbye, Ray," Tessa said. "Get home safe."

"Enjoy your evening, Tessa." Ray exited down the walk away from her office.

Tessa put on her light rain jacket and grabbed her purse and briefcase from the desktop. She glanced at her watch. The time read seven-fifteen. She wasn't sure if she wanted to be late meeting Jose, to show a little passive attitude, or if she should be the punctual school girl who's always on time, even to meet her seedy boyfriend at his job. The core of her didn't want to wait. A fire had been burning there for over a decade when she swore off men to raise her boy as a single mother. But Zachery was growing up. He needed her less and less each year. She had more of her life back again, and she wanted to spend that time with someone e, even if it was after hours at the workplace.

She heard a deep voice with a thick Southern Spanish accent when she stepped into the main office. He handled the simplicity of the English language with the grace of poetry, making the words sound foreign, even in their native dialect. Turning to her right, she saw Raoul approaching Robert Hamilton's office, and she instantly thought about Arlette. She wanted to call her and warn her. But there was nothing to warn her about. She couldn't be sure that anything would necessarily happen.

And why should that be any of my business? She thought.

Tessa took the elevator down three flights to the thirty-third floor and got off. Taking the left to the walkway leading to the security station for the upper floors, she tugged at the handle, expecting the door to be unlocked, but it wasn't. She turned back down the hall, leaned against the wall by the door, and began to think heavily about Arlette and what Ray had told her about Robert and Raoul. Then she pictured Raoul standing in the doorway of Rob's office with his tie dangling from his left hand, somehow looking menacing in all his good nature. There was something lascivious in his posture that shouldn't be trusted. She had gone out with him in group settings and would notice how awkward he was around women. Very hands-on with the men in the group. He wasn't close with anyone in the office, but he was a very successful sales representative with a stellar work reputation. There was just something about him that couldn't be trusted. She heard the dinging of the elevator, signaling the door opening.

Instinctively, she knew that it would be Jose coming around the corner, so she propped herself in a pose that suggested sexuality. Thankful it was indeed Jose. The smile he shined her way was enough to soothe the burn she held on to for more than a decade.

"Hey, Babe," Jose said.

"Hey." Said, Tessa.

CHAPTER 7
LETTIE UNHINGED

Arlette's body dropped to the tiled floor of the terrace, hard as a fresh bag of soil. Like a vase cracked open, she shattered, buckled over, and tumbled to pieces. The glass beneath her, chewing at her arms and parts of her right leg. She couldn't feel the glass biting into her naked arms and bare legs. Everything was numb except her mouth, which she found the consciousness to ask, "What did you say to me?" She knew it was true. She heard Tessa right. There were signs over the years she chose to ignore or question. Working. Worrying. Barren. Barren.

"I'm sorry, Arlette."

"Are you playing some kind of sick joke, Tessa?"

"Now, I know we have a truculent past, but I would never call you with something like this if it wasn't the truth."

"Don't tell her about the website!" The male voice through the receiver revitalized Arlette. It came in a whisper so quiet she almost couldn't make out what it said. It broke her from the haze and filled her with something sicker.

"Website?" She whispered.

"Yeah… he's…" Tessa stalled.

"Don't tell her…" The voice muffled that time, nearly inaudible, mouthed. Arlette got up from the deck floor. Glass shards fell off her body like sand from a beach day. Her bare feet stepped through the debris like it was just a bumpy surface, the glass embedding itself into the soles of her feet. Arlette listened intently to the silence as she got up. She hoped that one of them would say more about their adventurous hoax because this couldn't be true. Robert wouldn't be so stupid.

Did she even know what he was capable of? Who was Robert Hamilton anyway? Who had she married?

"Jose's computer geek friends created some website where they play obscene videos of people being recorded without their knowledge. You know—like surveillance videos. There was one with a woman who replaced the milk in the office break room with her breast milk. Just nasty…"

"Tessa, what the fuck does this have to do with Robert?"

"Yo, why you even tellin' her?" Arlette heard the man's voice again. It triggered something in her body, like a bolt of lightning in a storming cloud. His voice didn't sound like Robert's, but it reminded her of him and the countless men who'd lied to her and countless other women and girls around the world lied to daily.

"She thinks I'm lying. I want her to see for herself." She heard Tessa say.

Arlette was quiet. She was already in the house from the terrace, in the spare room where they kept the home offices and Robert's closet full of his things. She went straight to Robert's desk, where his home computer, a laptop, sat closed on the surface of an old-fashioned hardwood desk that Robert claimed was owned by his great-grandfather. It was the only piece of furniture Arlette let him keep when moving out of his apartment. She hated the garish, oversized monster, but she tried to understand the sentimental value - if it belonged to his great-grandfather - that is. She sat at the desk, opened the laptop calmly, and waited patiently for the web address. Both her knees were bloody, and some smaller shards of glass had embedded themselves into the skin of her bare legs. Her legs looked like two diamond trees. She couldn't feel anything while sitting at her husband's desk. It was as if she was waiting for something to manifest in her heart. But there was nothing inside a broken heart. Just a sad emptiness that was too familiar to shake away.

"Arlette."

"I'm here." A slight annoyance in her voice. She tapped the touchpad on the keyboard, and the screen opened. Rob was a stickler about cleanliness but was no genius at computers or passwords. His online life was quite messy and disoriented. Arlette liked that there was some tangible manifestation of her husband's imperfection. She cracked his password the first time she stayed the night at his apartment when they were just dating. She found nothing special there while he took another one of his long showers. There was a digital copy of a manuscript that Robert had never finished, of a screenplay he hoped to one day get produced. She read most of it throughout their courting. She didn't think it was any good at all. She didn't think he had talent as a writer, but she never told him to his face. What she found odd, checking his browser history, was the endless amount of porn he had been viewing on the internet. All the videos of threesomes or gang bangs of black women in rooms of white men. Some titles were so abusive they seemed personally offensive. Even then, she didn't know what to think of his sexual interests. He'd never express a desire to do any of the things he was watching in those explicit videos. But then, Robert expressed little interest in sex with her at all. She was always the one to initiate. Most nights, she was left unrequited.

"Good, sister girl," Tessa said. The assumed comradery put Arlette off. "You ready for this."

"I need to see for myself."

"Go to incognitovideo.com. Jose's screen name is Jazz Hands. On the left-hand side of the screen, you should see a row of videos. Look for the one with the title: Office Boys."

"I made that up," Jose said. Arlette cringed.

"This is all just stupid." She heard Tessa say.

"You act like it's my fault those fags are going at it like wild dogs." He said. "Look at them. Yo, Melvin was right. Those pussy boys like to be seen. Look at how the one dude is handling your girl's husband like he's some sort of rag doll. He's just throwing him around the room like a handball."

"Oh, my goodness," Tessa said in a low, distracted tone as if watching something. "Is he choking Rob? Oh. Arlette, honey, I don't think this is a good idea after all."

The computer took its sweet time loading the web page, but Arlette remained patient and didn't listen to Tessa's ruling on the matter. She had to know for herself if what they were saying was the truth. Her heart knew there was no other explanation for the neglect and distance throughout their marriage. This wasn't new. This was pending from the moment she got him the job at the mortgage company.

The web page finally loaded. Arlette found the video on the left side of the screen. She looked at the icon and, at first, couldn't make out the still picture above the name. It was dark except for a piercing bright office light in the center of the video, and as she fixed her sight on the image, it was clear there were two men in the picture. One tall, very muscular, and broad-shouldered man with wavy black hair. His white dress pants were down around his ankles. His black shirt was open, revealing his bulging muscular chest behind a white t-shirt. He towered over a smaller man with the swimmer's build and light-colored hair. His face turned from the camera, but Arlette could recognize the back of his head. There was a black string tied around the neck of the man she thought was Robert. It leads to the hand of the man standing over him. It looked like a tie being used as a dog leash. She circled the cursor around the picture, and to her horror, it moved. The man behind thrust and beat at her husband's ass like he was riding a bull in a rodeo. Then the face of the other man turned, revealing what she dreaded she'd see. Even in the black and white of the video, she could see the ecstasy in the stark blue eyes of the man she had married. She wanted to scream but couldn't. There wasn't even a gasp. Just a silent acknowledgment.

What are you gonna do, Arlette? She heard a voice clear as a whistle speak from somewhere in the claustrophobic room. But she was alone. It was a teasing, taunting sound that urged the rising violence in her spirit. That same voice urged defiance at her stepmother that day in the blistering sun of the backyard. That same rising violent urge made her defy her father and marry the man she decided, at that moment, she would kill.

But how, Arlette? The voice spoke up again as she stared at the pornographic image on display for the entire world wide web to see. *You can't just run up in there with an axe and slice his head open.* The voice giggled now, teasing at the idea like a light, off-colored joke. But Arlette was thinking just that beyond the voice. Somewhere in the black mist growing in her spirit as she stared at the video, afraid but tempted to run the cursor over it just one more time to watch the man choke Robert again, like the filthy dog he was to her now.

"Arlette, honey, are you still with me?" Tessa said. "I'm so sorry, sister."

"Stop calling me that!" Arlette snapped. She slammed the lid of the laptop down, got up from the desk and began pacing the room, holding the receiver to her ear, not sure why or what she should do. "I'm not your sister. We're barely friends."

"You don't like me because you think I'm jealous of you," Tessa said.

"I took your job."

"And you helped me to get a better one. One, that is better suited for me. So what if it was down the line a few years? You helped me. It's only right to look out for you. The way you did for me."

"I recommended you for the promotion to get you away from me. You were getting too close."

"Doesn't matter what you did it for," Tessa said. "What matters is what you did for me."

An axe, Arlette. Where would we get an axe this time of night?

"Tessa, I've got to go," Arlette said. She scrambled around the room, getting things together to leave the house. "You should tell your boyfriend he's breaking company policy by using private video on a public website. They're probably going to fire him when they find out." Arlette's voice was calm and official, as if managing a transaction.

"What are you going to do about Robert?" Tessa asked.

"Kill him."

"Please don't do something you will regret in the long run. Let me come to where you are."

"Wait, this is our date night!" The male voice said.

"Shut up, Jose. This is about sisterhood. I know what she's going through."

"You have no clue what I'm going through, girl!" Arlette screamed. She hurled the cell phone across the room and smashed a mirror hanging from the wall over her desk in the office. More shattering shards of glass spewed from the frame and seemed to leap out at Arlette like they wanted to cut at her black skin. The sound of the mirror bursting made an explosion that sounded like a rifle fired. A sharp shard did chance to skim Arlette's calve, but she didn't feel the cut or the blood that leaked down her leg.

With her car keys and bag, still in her working clothes, only disheveled now, torn, and messy from the late afternoon on the terrace, Arlette stormed out the front door of their condo, into the lonely hallway, to the empty elevator, into the quiet parking garage where she got into her car and drove off into the night.

CHAPTER 8
POST-COITUS

Rob's hands needed and rubbed at his neck while he paced the office along the area in front of the large bay window. He looked down into the city, trying to avoid looking at Raoul, who had helped himself to a seat behind Rob's desk. His pants were still down around his ankles, and he was playing with his now flaccid cock as if to soothe it. There was blackness all around them from the larger main office, and the massive, endless black sky grayed over now with thick circling clouds lumbering past his window. The clouds looked to have dying life inside of them.

Rob spat at Raoul. "Get your pants on!"

"That was fantastic, Robert," Raoul said. His accent sent a prickling chill up Rob's spine this time. He cringed and turned back to the misty night.

"Pull your pants up," Rob said again.

"You were real tight," Raoul said. Rob could see Raoul's reflection in the window, squeezing his cock and rereleasing it. He remembered the pain and the heat of the ecstasy. "I hope I didn't hurt you, Bud."

"Now, you're worried about that?" Rob said. He paced himself into the far corner of the office and looked out the window there. He felt like he was on the edge of the skyscraper, ready to jump into the black. His rectum ached. He always knew it would be painful, and Raoul had been so rough. Too rough. The punches would leave whelps, then bruises. How could he explain that to Arlette?

"You are walking a little differently," Raoul said. He stood up and let his cock dangle, semi-bulged and arrogant. He looked down at himself with a wide smile. "He gets me out of control sometimes, Rob. I'm sorry."

"Pull up your pants, Raoul!" Rob shouted. He turned slightly, then turned back to the window to avoid another encounter with the dick. The aching in his anus intensified when he entertained the thought another moment.

Raoul bent down to grab his pants. "Why are you being such a — ouch!" On his way up from the bend, he hit the back of his head on the bottom of the desk. "Ow! Damn, it! Rob!"

"You should watch what you're doing."

"You're being such a bitch." Raoul said, finally getting his pants up around his waist. "I was a little rough. You took it like a champ. Man up, Robert. Damn! No dude wants a pansy ass fag to fuck around with. Trust me. You'll get used to it."

"This won't happen again," Rob said. He wasn't so sure he believed his own words.

"Yeah, right!" Raoul said. He was buttoning his black shirt. The tie was still dangling from his wrist. "The wall's broken now, compadres; there's no turning back for you. You'll ache for it. In a good way, though. Trust me." Raoul shuffled over to Rob, who was nearly shaking by the window. He slapped Robert hard on his ass. Rob winced and scurried away from Raoul to reclaim his place at his desk.

"You really hurt me, Raoul. It might be serious." His voice sounded pleading as if he expected Raoul to have a cure like some lover would.

"See a doctor and send me a bill."

"We didn't use a condom."

"Listen. I'm clean. All right." Raoul's voice was confident. Rob had no choice but to believe him after what had already gone down. He shook his head. "Pull yourself together. I'm a little bigger than the average, Papito, I know. But you took me like you were from the streets…"

"We could get caught."

"That's the fun part." Raoul moved closer to Rob, slow and deliberate. Raoul's meer size intimidated Rob, but the feelings Manny evoked in him scared Robert even more. That uncontrollable sexual urge pulled them closer to Raoul like a magnet. He wanted to go again. Right there on the office floor without a care about what might happen if they did. He felt unleashed. Unbound by the weight of his heterosexual disguise. The feeling was insatiable.

He looked down at his watch to distract himself.

"It's a quarter to nine. I need to get home."

"I'm surprised the bulldozing, black bitch hasn't called here demanding you get your white ass home," Raoul said. "Hey! Does she make you the slave around the house as reparations for all those years they suffered?" He laughed in Rob's face.

"You're a sick piggie, Raoul," Robert said. His words were nearly inaudible.

Rob knew it was pointless to defend his wife's honor after shaming their marriage, sprawled out with a dick in his ass, over the desk she helped him to gain. He would look ridiculous. In another way, he felt relieved that the thing had finally come to a head and burst into existence with no possibility of turning back. The fear of making a last passage through the misery he created with Arlette to explore the life he once thought taboo had melted with harsh heat. There was no place to return.

Raoul was upright and fully dressed when Rob looked at him again. The black shirt still revealed the top portion of his hairy, bulging chest just enough to appear concealed. The impression of his quiet cock still pressed against his pant leg. It was less of a threat satiated. Tiny details of the sex flashed through Rob's mind as he stood in the middle of the office, trying not to look at Raoul but needing to look all the same. The punching and the hard whacking of his ass cheeks - particularly the right one, the wild grunting sounds that were like wolves or wild bears, at moments. What cavemen must have sounded like centuries ago when they discovered sex in the wild. He remembered the dominance and craved it no matter how it hurt. Then he shook his head hard to push the memories aside.

"Button the rest of your shirt, Raoul. We need to get out of here."

"Why don't you call that bitchy black wife of yours and tell her you're not coming tonight? Tell her I got you drunk – a matter of fact–here's an idea–why don't we go out, get wasted, and then head back to my hotel? All on the company card. We can call the bitch when we land in the bed, Robbie. Then only half of what you tell her is a lie." Raoul had moved into the center of the office to be face-to-face with Rob. Rob could smell the sultry scent of the sex they had on the desk, like a dying flower between them. An enticing aroma that drew him into Raoul like a moth to light.

"You're out of your mind," Rob said. He was calm and still. His voice even.

"You're saying you're down?"

"Button your shirt."

Raoul undid the buttons of his black shirt, starting at the bottom. His eyes locked with Rob's as they stood in the room's pit, feeling the black world cover them. Raoul's shirt was fully open again, and his hands were by his side. To Rob, he looked like a Goliath, tamed by desire and slave to the flesh. He could not understand why or how he had become the object of this affection, but he refused to reject the opportunity.

"Touch me," Raoul said.

"No," Rob said.

"You can touch me, Rob." Raoul insisted. "I want you to."

Robert timidly stepped in closer, bridging the slight gap between them. The male sex scent grew stronger. A gush of wind slapped the bay window, causing it to shake slightly, giving them both a start. They grabbed for one another. Pulling into an embrace. Rob's face is buried in the forest of Raoul's chest hairs. He bathed in the glory of their manhood. He couldn't remember in his adult life ever feeling so content and complete. He laughed into Raoul's chest.

Raoul rested his head on the top of Rob's and softly laughed into Rob as he held him in a mighty bear hug.

"I'm sorry I hurt you, Robbie," Raoul said.

Rob could not speak. He wiggled his way out of Raoul's grip to scale down his body to his core. There, he unzipped Raoul's pants and reached inside the folds for his slightly erect cock. Rob did not speak. He went to work on his desires yet again.

Chapter 9
I WANT YOU TO TAKE IT DOWN, JOSE!

"Yo, what was that sound?" Jose said through a small, breathy laugh. His eyes never left the wall of monitors in front of the desk in the tight security surveillance room. "Did your friend just blow her brains out over this faggot?" He pointed at the screen where the image of Robert and Raoul played out their sexual tryst.

"Jose, don't call him that. That's rude and disrespectful."

"I'm rude and disrespectful? When this dick catcher is sprawled out over a desk in a corporate office, letting that gringo play pool up in his…"

Tessa whacked him hard on his arm.

"Ouch, girl!" Jose screamed. "Be wrong if I hit you back, right?"

"Yes, it would be. Just as wrong as your foul mouth. The one I'm getting tired of for one night." Tessa said. She was frantically scrolling through her phone, trying to find Arlette's number again. "I want you to take that video down, Jose."

"I ain't taking shit down," Jose said. Tessa looked down at him from her cell phone like a mother with a switch cut clean from a bush. "What you lookin' at me like that for?" Jose said. "You ain't my Mama. There are over six thousand people across the world watching this live stream right now. I ain't taking it down. That's my word. Dem two shoulda known betta." Jose said, looking indignant. Tessa wanted to smack the expression onto the floor, make him pick it up, and put it back on his face so she could smack it off again. It was Jose's arrogance that turned her from him at times.

"I said, take the video down," Tessa demanded, going back to her phone. "I've got to try Arlette until I get a hold of her. She can't be all right."

"Yo, I think your friend offed herself."

"Shut up, Jose. And take that damn video off that website. I can see you're still streaming it live. Take it down, now!" Tessa said. She whacked him on the arm a second time.

"I ain't."

"What did you just say to me?"

"I ain't takin' shit down. This video is already up to six thousand views, and it's only been up for an hour." Jose said. "I'm thinking it's going viral. Them dudes are assed out." He burst into a peal of uncontrollable hysterical laughter that had a hard-wheezing sound penetrating through his lungs. Tessa narrowed her eyelids to where the brown showed through narrow snake-eyed slits. She hated the gossipy side of her lover. It brought out the cowardice in him so much so that he reminded her more of a fat gossip than a romantic Latino with a few extra pounds. Tessa had seen this side of her man more often than she liked to remember, and each time was worse. Watching him now, drooling over the monitors, his oversized shoulders bulking, laughing as he extended a sausage-like finger to the computer screen pointing at the two men sexing - nearly made her dry heave. His disposition was so repulsive it made him sexually unattractive. He looked pitiful and hypercritical. A hurt person with nothing better to do than hurt someone else.

"I think I should call the cops," Tessa said.

"No, Cheeka! Stay out of it. It's not your place. You've done enough already."

"I'm going to tell them about your little internet scheme. I think you should take it down now, Jose. You've had enough fun at someone else's expense."

"Doesn't look like these two finished yet, Cheka. Look." He said, pointing at the monitor to the far right. The computer screen image was delayed by several minutes and did not capture what Jose and Tessa saw on the surveillance camera monitor.

Rauol had Rob pinned to the window wall from behind as he thrust his pelvis hard against his buttocks and punched at Rob's ribs. He slapped violently at Rob's naked thighs. Then he took Rob by the neck and hurled him to the floor of the office. Rauol forced Rob's face into the carpet floor while he thrust violently into him, pounding Robert's backside with no mercy. Tessa had to turn away from the monitor. Jose watched the action like it was a kickboxing fight.

"This is crazy," Tessa said. Frantically, she scrolled through her phone again for Arlette's number, trying to understand why it wasn't just in the call log. "Where is that number?"

"These dudes are like animals. How is your boy taking that shit like that?" Jose's question seemed genuine.

"Jose, I said take it down. I'm leaving, and I'm going to the other security guys and tell them what you're doing up in here."

"Melvin knows about that Florida dude."

"What?"

"Yeah. He set this up. He told me to catch that Florida dude on camera."

"This is crazy." Tessa's jaw dropped.

"Why are you going off about that Arlette chick when she stole your job? Didn't they make her manager over you? Why you feel you owe that bitch? This is some instant karma shit if you ask me."

She nearly smacked Jose, but she knew if she hit hard enough across his face, he'd strike her back. Jose was a man, after all. Wasn't he? And a vain gossip. She held the phone tighter in her hand and stared down at him.

"I don't see it that way, Jose. I think I should go."

"Nah." Jose turned from the monitors and put his hand on Tessa's arm to stop her from leaving. "You should try your friend again. Don't leave." He sounded humbled.

Tessa looked down at the phone, and to her surprise, Arlette's number was at the top of the call list. "I found it!" She tapped the name on the screen, and the cell phone rang on the open line. Jose quickly turned back to the monitors and his video streaming. Tessa turned away from him, shaking her head.

"Hello… Arlette… Thank God! Girl, I was so worried… What was that loud noise?" there was silence in the tiny boxed room. The bulky workstation cluttered the room, leaving little floor space to move around. It was hard for Tessa to get as far away from Jose as she wanted to. Then her pacing stopped. She stood in the center of the room with the phone hard pressed against her ear. Her face flushed a dark pink in her light brown skin. Her big brown eyes widened and swelled with tears as she listened.

Disturbed by her silence, Jose turned to find Tessa's face wet with tears, and she was quietly sobbing. He got up from his seat, nearly snatching the phone from her. He could hear Arlette scream on the other end of the line. Tessa put the phone on speaker and held it out between them.

"… you sorry, bitch. I am not your fucking friend. And your Mexican boy toy should turn in his security badge tonight because he's about to lose his J.O.B. by the time I am through with him. I hope you are listening in, Chico. She got me on the speaker yet?"

"Fuck you, Fag Hag, Bitch!" Jose screamed. Tessa put her hand to his mouth and gave him a dirty look that calmed him instantly.

"Tess, I know you can't wait to get to work tomorrow and tell all them bitches in your coffee clutch what a Cornhole my husband is and how stupid I was to marry him…"

"Arlette, I wouldn't do that. I don't know why you think I could do something like that." Tessa said through a sob.

"Yeah. Sure, you're right. Well, I got an even bigger scandal for your asses. You and your burrito boy toy." Arlette's voice lowered, "Just keep your eyes glued to that surveillance screen cause you about to get the show of the century."

"It's already a grand slam, Cheeka," Jose said. Tessa shot another look. He quieted.

"Keep on talking, Gringo." Arlette hissed. "Cause your whole scam is about to go viral. You ready to raise the roof?"

"Hell, yeah!" Jose screamed back.

"Shut up, Jose," Tessa said. "Arlette, what do you mean by that? What are you about to do? Where are you, girl?"

Through the cell phone line, they could hear mumbling sounds like a transaction at a cash register. There was loud nineties music playing in the background. It sounded like Arlette had just laid the phone on the counter while she worked out the transaction. They heard a woman's voice shout, "Good luck with cutting down that tree!" before the phone line went dead.

Jose looked up at Tessa's wet, flushed face and wanted to kiss her. But he was afraid. He asked, "You still want me to take it down, Cheeka?"

CHAPTER 10
LETTIE AT THE WAYMART

Racing through the aisle of the semi-crowded late-night Waymart shopping world in downtown Brooklyn, Arlette looked to be in a desperate search for a lost treasure or a winning lottery ticket when, in fact, she was looking for the gardening section. She had been there once before with Robert when he was on one of his 'naturalizing the terrace' Sunday afternoons. During a quiet breakfast that Sunday morning, she got the idea in her head that she'd make this a couples outing and join Robert on his folly of wooding up the terrace.

"It'll be our own private forest in the sky." He shouted excitedly when she told him she would join him on his trip to the Waymart. Her initial thought was: *Why do you work outside of work hours? And hard labour at that?* But she didn't want to come across as condescending as Robert had accused her of being in the past. That Sunday morning, she thought to herself, *What the heck? How hard could gardening be? He'll do most of the heavy lifting.* What could she lose?

Rob had known exactly where the garden section was. All she had to do was follow close behind. She dragged herself through the isles with slumped shoulders, trailing a pepped stepping Robert, more than eager to get to the shrubbery and plant section. He didn't even notice—or perhaps didn't care—that Arlette's enthusiasm for the outing had already fizzled to a fart that stank harder than the bags of soil lining the aisles.

Finally arriving at the gardening section, it shocked Arlette to see Robert race to where the trees gathered like a mini-forest in the large Waymart display. *Oh, He's serious.* She thought as she stopped following, straightening her back as a clerk breezed by her to greet Robert like a shark sniffing blood. Robert pointed out to the clerk the assortment of trees he was looking to buy and inquired about the sort of pots he should get and how many bags of soil to buy. Arlette teased herself with the idea of the countless hours out on the terrace working like a slave in the blistering sun of Robert's garden haven. The whole time waiting for Massa to say it was time to eat and they could go inside.

That's when Arlette imagined Emma at the doorway of their terrace like a guard refusing to let her inside, away from the sun's oppressive heat. The vision came to her as clear as that faithful day long ago in the backyard of her childhood home. She carried that feeling of fiery rage with her as Robert shopped for all the items they would need to lug up to the penthouse and then drag out onto the terrace. All the while tracking dirt through every crevasse, dirt will gather. Then, the work would begin on the hot balcony.

When they got to the counter to pay for all the items, a glass-encased shelf stood between the patron and the cashier. It displayed several tools for gardening. Arlette stared into the case, trying to avoid the bill they had racked up on Robert's lofty Sunday excursion. Then, a handy item caught her eye. It lay nestled in the far left corner of the display shelf. An axe with a sky-blue handle and a sharp blade seemed to glisten against the top light of the shelf. It spoke to Arlette. *With* me, *you could cut those trees down a week after he plants them in the pots,* It said. The voice had a subtle hiss, like a rattlesnake low enough that only she could hear, and in that moment, it was all she could hear. It went on. *Perhaps I could even end up buried in the back of his head.* It laughed so loud that Arlette had to shake herself to keep from laughing with it.

"Lettie!" Robert called out. Lettie was a name he had reserved for when he was in a splurging mood. Teasing her with a nickname only her father could use. He knew how it pulled at her heartstrings. "What are you doing way over there?"

Don't forget me. Arlette heard the axe say as she turned back to her husband to join him at the other end of the counter.

"Got everything we need," Arlette spoke through a false smile, one that even the clerk could see through.

Scrambling through the aisles now, an inner voice sounded like the axe guiding her through the rows of housewares, toiletries, and personal products until she arrived at the back of the massive store, at the garden area, that couldn't be missed.

Lawnmowers were parked at the entrance, delineating the gardening section. Various brands and sizes of machines were on display, reminiscent of a front lawn in a suburban neighbourhood with a white picket fence. Arlette felt the urge to rearrange them, to disrupt the perfect image they portrayed. Passing by the last mower on her right, she nudged it with her foot, knocking the proud machine out of its pristine spot. This minor act provided a small dose of satisfaction to her soul.

Arlette looked haggard in her torn work clothes and her hair dishevelled. The long locks were frayed and spewed about her head and body like a wet net cast too many times overboard to catch fish. The blood on her knees from the broken glass had dried in crusted lines past her knees. She still felt nothing but rage. Driving downtown, she was quiet and cautious of the road. Maneuvering through the traffic with much care. She didn't listen to music as she would typically do. She was listening for it, that voice. She could hear it in her head like an echo of the last time she heard it, but not the way she had back in the condo. Then, it sounded like someone was in the home office with her. It would come again like a piano dropping from a ten-story building. It would come again. Arlette was prepared to listen. She heard it when she got out of the car in the parking lot.

You came for me. It said. Arlette speed-walked through the lot, into the entrance, and up the aisle to the gardening section.

Her eyes darted from the water hose to window screens and racks of seeds and soil. The rows had an isolated scent of manure that reminded Arlette of that hot spring day on the terrace with Rob. A few minutes after getting started on their 'Garden in the Sky', after hauling all the materials out of the rental truck, into the condo, and out onto the terrace, Arlette decided it was time for a break and went inside for gin and lemonade and never returned to the terrace. Rob remained outside until the work was complete. He never once came inside. Not even to use the bathroom. If he had, he'd have found Arlette passed out on the bed, exhausted. They never tried gardening again. It became Robert's passion.

Something else pulling them in different directions. Arlette was thankful for the time away from him, but at the same time, the attention and the tenderness with which Robert took care of his plants made her see red with jealousy. Even if he had tried, Lettie would have spurned his advances. *I played my part in this, too*. It was her own voice she heard in her head at that time.

Before she could feel sorry for her marriage, Arlette found the glass counter where the store held its more dangerous gardening tackle. That same glass counter where she first met her tool of choice. And there he was. Bright silver in blue handle glory. The sharp, icy blade glistened at her like the day they met. Like a sparkle of a freshly cleaned smile. *Lettie. You came back for me.*

"Looking to cut down an unwanted tree?" A squeaking, bubbled voice gayly sounded from the other side of the counter. It snapped Arlette upright, and she stepped half an inch from the glowing counter.

"You could say that." She said, flashing a stiff smile at the clerk. The girl looked homely and only twenty years old. Her flat brown hair was pulled back into a ponytail with a part in the middle. Her face was long, like her torso. She looked like an odd bird perched on a branch with her slim fingers crossed on the countertop.

Arlette thought, for the first time since she left the condo, what she might look like to the outside world. She abruptly remembered the traumatizing moment on the terrace when she fell to the floor. For a moment, she felt the pain of her body smacking the cement floor and her knee crushing the glass—she felt the sting of the cuts then. But the voice ceased the start of the pain when it called out to her again. This time again, using the familiar *Lettie...* to beckon her.

"How much for this item here?" She said, pointing to the blue handle of the axe, her hand hovering over it. She felt the strength of its power like a magnet drawing her touch.

"I'd have to check in the back to see if we have it in stock."

"But there is one here—in the case. I'll take this one."

"That's the display. We try not to sell the display for return purposes. There's no packaging."

"I don't mind."

"Let me just check in the back. We may have the axe, packed, in stock."

"You have one here." Arlette tapped the top surface of the glass case with a hard-painted nail. The sound seemed large enough to crack or scratch the glass top.

The clerk's back stiffened, and she stepped an inch back from the counter. "I'll be right back." She said to Arlette's stone glare. She had no intention of opening that counter without checking the stock room first. Arlette, too, could see it in the girl's eyes. The clerk was frightened of what she might do with the open axe if she handed it over to her. She threw on her phoney smile again. This time, trying to seem overtly believable.

"Of course. You should check." Arlette said.

The clerk retreated to the storage area with a quick and stern look at Arlette before disappearing behind the dividing wall. Arlette's obscene smile fell back into the grimace she brought into the store. Her cell phone buzzed around in her oversized black handbag. She snatched the bag from the closet when she left the condo because it was perfect for concealing an enormous weapon, yet stylish enough to go unnoticed amongst New York's fashionistas. There was no reason to enter the workplace looking like a deranged, bitter wife about to slash her husband and his Gay Latin lover into bits. She could cover the cuts on her knees with the bag should security examine her or begin to ask questions. Perhaps Melvin—her smoking buddy—would be on duty tonight. He'd let her in without question.

She tossed the vibrating bag onto the counter to dig for her wallet and the buzzing cell phone. She fished the cell phone out first. The call she missed was from a local number she didn't recognize. Soon after contemplating the digits, the phone buzzed again, showing a message had been left. She started to call the voicemail when another call came through. This number had a name attached to it. The caller was Tessa.

Arlette answered the call in a tirade of offensive obscenities aimed at her co-worker, and the patrons in the nearby aisles moved away quickly, shaking their heads and covering their ears. Arlette didn't care what they thought. She saw them all with their disparaging glares and spit fire back at them with her own stares. They would just call her crazy and go about their day with another one lost. What did they care? And now, what did she care? She turned her stare back to the shining axe in the glowing cabinet and felt as calm as the blue of the handle. The silver blade was as crisp as a harp string.

The clerk returned toward the calming of Arlette's rant. Arlette's back was to her. "Ma—Mam—Miss…" Arlette turned quickly and put the phone on the counter, pointing a determined fingernail at the blade, hammering the glass case.

"I want this blade." She said through grinding teeth. The clerk looked up from Arlette's demands and saw the other patrons gathering in the aisle, pretending not to notice the outburst. She nodded at them from behind the counter and was sure to smile. This gesture seemed to put everyone at ease. She giggled a little when she spoke to Arlette in a calm salesperson's voice.

"That's great. You're in luck because we are clear out in the back, and if you want it, I'll have to sell you the display. Let me get that out and wrap it in some bags so you won't cut yourself." The clerk pulled the axe from the display case. She wrapped the blade carefully in several Waymart plastic bags. Arlette fumbled through her purse for her wallet while the cell phone lay on the counter in an open call. She watched the silver blade disappear behind the plastic bags like she was watching a Christmas gift unwrapped and then wrapped again. The clerk finally scanned the barcode at the tip of the axe handle and the item rung up to:

"Thirty-seven ninety-five. Will that be cash or charge?" The clerk asked. The gardening area was peaceful again.

"Arlette!" A screeching voice whizzed through the open cell phone line on the counter. Arlette snatched up the phone and pressed it against her chest. Eventually, she tossed it in the bag with the call still open. The clerk dismissed these actions with a waiting, fakevsmile and an overly patient exhale. Arlette fished a credit card from the wallet and handed it to the clerk.

"Charge, please. No receipt." The clerk ran the card and handed it back to Arlette. She thought she could hear the muffled sounds of the caller in the black bag. The aisles were clear of people. The clerk was there alone with Arlette. She still held the blade-wrapped axe on her side of the counter, waiting for the card to go through.

"You're approved." The clerk said, handing the axe to Arlette, who took it by the handle like a prize trophy and stuffed it into the oversized black bag like a thief. "Thank you for shopping at Waymart. You're all set. And good luck chopping down that tree." The clerk shouted the last part after Arlette, who was already down the aisle, heading for the exit, to her car in the lot, speeding out into the night traffic as the sky blackened with menacing storm clouds brewed a hard rain to fall in the wicked night.

She could hear the muffled cackling of the blade loud and clear in the car's cabin as she sped through the streets of downtown Brooklyn. She went over to the bridge into lower Manhattan, pushing toward the Liberty and Broadway office.

Ha, Ha, Ha, Ha, Ha, Ha, Ha, Ha, Ah-Ah-Ah-Ah Ha, Ha, Ha, Ha, Ha, Ha, Ha, Ha, Ah-Ah-Ah-Ah

CHAPTER 11
POST COITUS ROUND TWO

Rob stared into the picturesque black sky outside his grand window, sitting in his office chair behind his desk, lost in the haze. Those glowing lights in the city below him were dimmer now from the clouds collecting like a thick, creamy roux. The traffic moving over the bridge had simmered to a few cars. They crossed the bridge with ease on that quiet night just before a severe storm would break.

Rob's shirt was open again. His pants were up around his waist, zipped but unfastened. He stared into the reflection of Raoul, dressing again. Raoul was staring at himself in the window wall facing the office area. He posed for empty cubicles as if there was a phantom audience to witness his twisted role-playing. He paraded boastfully, with no sign of shame for his violence. As if to say: 'The faggots like it hard. They beg for it that way.' When he finally zipped his fly, he shifted his balls under the crotch of his zipper. Rob shook his head and rolled his eyes.

Their second bat at lovemaking was more complicated than the first. Rob felt the pain of the brutal sex more than the first time. *There will be bruises for sure.* He was worn out. It hurt to sit, but nothing else could ease the soreness.

"I tested negative this year - for HIV. If that's your problem." Raoul said over his shoulder. Still admiring his image in the reflection cast back to him in the black of the empty room.

"That's not the problem," spoke Rob. It was a burst unexpected by both men.

"Then what is it with the radio silence, Robert? You acted like you wanted it this time."

"You didn't even give me a warning."

"I thought you'd be into it. You seemed so hungry."

"Not like—no!" Rob turned back to the window. There were tears in his eyes he didn't want Raoul to see.

"Oh, get over yourself, pussy boy. You'll go back to your bitchy black wife and your fucked-up straight life and fantasize about this night every time she's away on some business trip. Should the mood hit you, and I'm in town, hit me up." Raoul laughed a hideous, vulgar sound that made Rob wince. Raoul turned into the room to hit the back of the visitor's chair for emphasis.

"What's with the torment, Raoul? You can go now that you marked your turf,"

"Trying to put me out now, huh? I think I'll stay and watch you squirm a little longer. There might just be a round three."

"This will never happen again."

"Oh, come on. This isn't the first time, and I sure as hell won't be the last guy. You liked it too much." Raoul grabbed his crotch and thrust his hips into the space between them. With Rob watching, he thrusted out a little more. He looked like a foul and overstuffed Michael Jackson impersonator.

"Why are you so cold about this?" Rob asked as he got up from the chair to fasten his pants. He turned to Raoul but wouldn't look him in the eye. "Did this mean anything at all to you?" He whispered as if he were afraid a ghost would hear and pass on the news.

"Stop acting like that!"

"Like what?" Rob pleaded.

"Like that. Like a bitch. You sound like a fucking bitch." Raoul said. "Man up, Robert. We're guys having a little fun after work. That's all this could ever be. You're married—for fuck's sake."

"I'll have to divorce Arlette. I can't sleep with her now. Not again." Rob said those words more to himself than he meant to be heard. They were affirmations of the following steps he would need to take to live as his true self. Robert knew there was no possibility of a genuine relationship with Raoul. He wasn't altogether convinced that the Gays were capable of commitment. There were so many choices. "I thought-"

"What? That I was going to get down on one knee and propose to you after tossing your goods upside down across your desk? No thanks, Robbie baby. You were just another conquest. A notch on the belt—I think, as the saying goes."

The office phone rang so loud in the silence that it seemed to bounce off the glass walls like a bright red rubber ball. Raoul and Rob stood on opposite sides of the desk facing one another, with the phone ringing between them. The call indicator light blinks the unanswered line.

"You'd better answer that," Raoul said. "I'm sure it's the ball and chain calling. Wondering why your cheating ass isn't at home yet. I'm gonna go. This entire scene is looking more pathetic by the hour."

"Raoul, please don't leave me like this." Rob couldn't catch the words before they spilt from his mouth. In the instant after saying them, he could hear the pitiful pleading in his voice and suddenly felt sorry for his soul. Even with a shattered heart, he couldn't let this triumphant moment in the growth of his sexuality expire.

"You want to go it a third time?" Raoul said, his mouth twisting into a sardonic grin as one side of his mouth lifted and a dark brow raised, hinting at a genuine question. "I thought I was too rough for you."

The phone line incessantly buzzed beneath their exchange. Rob had no intention of answering it. It was after hours. What should anyone want at this ungodly hour? Arlette was the only employee he knew who took the job home every night. He raised an open hand to Raoul to stop him from leaving.

"Hold on." He said. "Please, Raoul." Rob snatched the phone from the receiver. "Hello."

"I knew you were still at the office,"

"Arlette. Hey… I had a last-minute meeting with Raoul from the Florida office. We lost track of time."

"Hm." Rob could hear whooshing sounds in the background, like she was in a car with the windows down.

"Where are you?"

"Outside on the terrace. Our Own Private Garden in the Sky. Isn't that what you named it?"

"Yeah." Rob smiled at the memory of that moment on the terrace. He bragged to her about the progress of all his hard work. The terrace was lovely. She had even admitted to that. Even after she abandoned the project. "I did."

"You know, there's always noise on the streets below at this hour. It's bustling tonight. I'm leaning over the edge of the divider. I never noticed how far down it was from here. The world almost seems upside down."

"Arlette, you sound strange," Robert frowned. "I want you to get off the terrace. Don't lean over the edge like that. I don't like when you do that."

"You remember that?"

"Why wouldn't I remember something you did just last week?" Rob looked up at Rauol, making his way to the office door. He shouldered the phone and frantically waved both hands to get Rauol's attention. He turned to face Rob, shrugging his shoulders and raising his eyebrows with outstretched palms.

"What do you want me to do?" He mouthed. "I've got to go." He hissed.

"Arlette, can I call you back? I need to wrap up with Raoul. I'll be home before midnight."

"It's already eleven, Robert," Arlette said. Her voice was more calm than usual, almost unsettling. It made Robert take pause. "Take your time, Rob. I called to let you know I would call it a night. I wanted to hear your voice before the day closed."

"You're sounding strange. I'll be home soon." He put the receiver back on the bed before she could respond. In a trance, he lunged past his desk with his hand reaching for Rauol.

"I don't want us to end like this." Desperately reaching for Rauol's hand or his cock, he wasn't sure which. He was met with a swatting slap in the same hand Rauol used to spank his ass. He snapped back from Robert.

"I told you to quit it with the girly show, Robert," Raoul said. "I'm not into you like that."

The phone buzzed in again.

"What the hell!?" Raoul said. "Is your line the twenty-four-hour emergency mortgage FAQ?"

"It's probably Arlette calling back." Rob went back to his desk to answer the line. He turned back to watch Manny wait. He hoped he wouldn't leave. "Arlette?" He said into the receiver.

"No. Rob. It's me, Tessa. The new manager for the Central Region. My office is right down the way from yours."

"Who are you? Tessa?" Rob said. A curiosity sprouts across his face. "You trained Arlette. The two of you were friends. Before she met me."

"Yes."

"Why are you calling my office so late? It's eleven o'clock."

"Listen, man, I'm out of here," Raoul said, turning to the door.

"Tell Raoul he should stay," Tessa said.

"What? How did you know he was here?" Raoul stopped and turned to Rob.

"I can see you through the security camera in the elevator bank," Tessa said. "We saw everything that happened. It's all on surveillance video, Rob."

Rob's face went void of all colour. His expression dropped with his jaw as he stared through the wall of glass, through the empty cubicle work area, and into the elevator bank. The black mirror bubble on the ceiling that encased the security camera stared back at him like a gigantic black eye in the sky.

Raoul ran to his side just before Robert dropped the phone to the ground and fainted. He sat him down in the executive chair behind the desk. Rob woke quickly to stare into the window of the black sky.

"What the hell is going on, Robert?" Raoul put the receiver to his ear. "Who the hell is this?"

"Raoul, you don't know me, but I now know too much about you," Tessa said. "I just told Rob that the security camera caught your sex acts on tape. And his wife knows about everything. I think she's on her way down to the office. I'm not sure, but I think she bought a weapon at the Waymart, and she's headed down here."

"What the hell are you talking about?" Raoul said.

"Oh, no!" Tessa said. "Arlette is in the lobby talking to security."

"What are you talking about? Rob just spoke to Arlette. She was at the condo."

Robert snapped out of his trance and hit the speaker phone indicator on the office phone bed.

"She's in the lobby right now talking to security." He heard Tessa's voice blaring through the phone intercom. The sound of her voice and the news it supported made him cringe.

A burst of lightning filled the sky outside and a booming hammer of thunder barreled the air behind the light. Raoul and Robert start at the illustrious sight and sound of the brooding storm outside. Tessa screamed into the receiver: "Arlette is in the building, Robert. She knows everything."

CHAPTER 12
BACK TO WORK

When she pushed through the revolving door of One Liberty Plaza, Arlette noticed the time was a quarter after eleven on the enormous clock behind the security desk. Arlette carried in with her a slight mist from the approaching rain outside. The bottoms of her flat shoes were wet and squeaked as she walked along the marble floor. The rain hadn't started up just yet, but there was a warning drizzle ushering in the pending downpour. The high ceiling in the cavernous lobby elevated the volume of her squeaking shoes to concert level. The loud noise caught the security guard's attention at the long desk. He stood up to face her. She was already at the turnstile, fishing through the large black bag for her access card to get through the turnstile.

"Arlette?" The security guard called out to her. She heard his call as if she had never heard her name before that moment. It sounded foreign as if it belonged to someone else. She almost looked over her shoulder when she finally lifted her face to meet the security guard. At first, she stared into the big man like she had never seen him before. He was too large to be a friend she would want or even remember an encounter with. *How could he know my name and speak it*

146

as if we were old college chums? She quickly assessed her bad habits without a clue, and his face became recognized.

"Melvin!" she said. "Hey. I can't seem to find my badge." She stopped rummaging through the black bag and pushed it behind her back to conceal the ax head bulging through the left corner. It was like the ax wanted to be seen. Perhaps she would act sooner. Give it a test run before the last kill. "I did something stupid. Stupid me. I left my house keys on my desk and can't find my key card to get through the turnstile..."

"Your husband is here late too..."

"Husband?" Those damn smoke breaks. She remembered wearing the ring out in front of the building while smoking with Melvin. In a moment of over-excitement, she thought there would be no harm in telling him who she had married. "Right. Robert *is* here. I suppose I could call up to him and have him..."

"I saw him with Rauol–your company representative from the–I forget what office."

"The Florida office. Yes, well, I'd better call up." With the wind blowing out of her sail, Arlette had a moment to recognize just how foolish her plan had been. Did she truly expect to stroll into her place of work and chop up her husband and his lover into little pieces right in his office without getting caught? The ax alone should have set off a hidden metal detector. She clenched the covered blade of the ax through the leather bag. That touch filled her with a burst of confidence. It called to her to snatch it out of the bag and do away with Melvin's meddling. But then something remarkable happened.

"I can help you, Mrs. Hamilton." He called her by her married name. That was something she didn't tell him. Robert's last name. How did he know that? "I'm sorry. Do you prefer Ms. Silver at the workplace?" Melvin's mouth rose into a knowing smile that seemed to read through her diary of thoughts in one lightning-fast moment. He saw her pain.

"Silver is what I prefer, Melvin," Arlette said. "I would appreciate the help. Thank you. I would hate to bother Mr. Hamilton with something so minor." She smiled at the middle-aged security guard, genuinely this time. Melvin reached into the breast pocket of his white button-down shirt, pulled a key card from it, and presented it to Arlette as if she had won a golden ticket. Her smile brightened in a sinister amusement. Her eyes glistened at the sight of the flat white card. A lock of her disheveled, long black hair settled along her face, reminding her of how disheveled she must have looked. It didn't seem to matter to Melvin. His welcome bordered trickery, and she wondered if this was all a setup. Her mind raced with every conspiracy theory she could think of. The ax pressed against her back through the leather bag, pointy end up. It felt like it was branding its shape into her back. It yearned for release.

Melvin delicately placed the card on the entry pad like he was doing a magic trick as Arlette's eyes hungrily watched the swirling motions. The partition bars were divided, opening an entryway into the elevator bank. It was the force of the ax that booted Arlette through the entrance. *Freedom, Lettie. Give us freedom.*

"You'd better hurry along, Ms. Silver," Melvin said with a distorted, broad smile plastered on his face. It was clown-like to Arlette. She hated clowns.

"Thank you, Melvin." She felt the need to apologize but couldn't. "I can't believe how forgetful I've become…"

"Marriage does that to you, Mrs. Hamilton." He said as the partition bars snapped back in place. "It will make you forget you exist if you let it. One gets so motivated by companionship that one forgets about one's own needs. Would you agree, Mrs. -"

"Ms. Silver." She said. "I prefer Arlette Silver. Mr. Rodriguez. Thank you again."

"Oh, anytime, anytime."

For a moment, she wondered if Melvin had seen the video of the brutal sexual act taking place in the office above his head. He had access to the cameras, just as Tessa's boyfriend did. He seemed too eager to assist her distressful circumstance. Melvin was kind but strict about building security. This was certainly out of protocol. Arlette didn't want to question the stroke of luck. The heat of the ax wouldn't let her do that. Not when they were so close.

"It was really no problem," Melvin said as the double doors to the elevator in front of Arlette opened. Strangely enough, Melvin used the key card to let himself into the elevator bank to face Arlette before the doors closed. He said, "If you run into your husband upstairs, please tell him I said 'hello.' A charming man he is."

"Charming? Yes." Arlette repeated in a daze, smiling blankly at Melvin's large, round body. For a moment, it looked like he had grown horns, bat wings, and a tail with an arrow pick at the end. Then, suddenly, the vision vanished. The elevator doors divide them. The ax burned hotter against her back.

CHAPTER 13
SECURITY!

Melvin Rodriguez can't remember when he'd ever had a friend. Growing up in Miami, FL, was difficult for him. Being around all the hard bodies and beautiful girls that frequent the beaches, his dad would take him to go fishing when he couldn't find work. He called it his way of bringing home the bacon when the grease in the pan was dry. His father - Melvin's grandad - walked out on his family before Melvin's father could get to know him well enough to have some memory of the man. Melvin's father watched his mother single-handedly raise himself and six siblings. Somewhere in all those years alone, he vowed never to do such a thing to his own children. His father stuck to that promise, and when his son, Melvin, was born into the world. His wife, the mother of his beloved son, died during childbirth, and he spent the rest of his life taking good care of his only boy.

The road was rough. They struggled during those early years when his father had to find work and someone to care for his boy while he worked. Someone he could trust.

Melvin's first memory of anyone closer to him other than his father was a woman he'd learned to call Aunt D. By the time he was five and in school, she was the person picking him up and bringing him home to her apartment until his father picked him up after working all day at whatever odd job he could find. Melvin and his father lived in the unfinished basement beneath the same building. There were leaks even when it didn't rain, and there was a problem with the air conditioner, but it was home for the most part. Melvin spent most of his adolescence there until his father got a better job as a security guard at a popular department store in the downtown area.

They moved into the apartment above Aunt D's then. Melvin had his own room. A door he could shut at night as he grew into the need for privacy. Walls were separating the living quarters and no leaks. The AC worked every time it was on. Melvin turned juvenile there, entering high school to make way for himself in the world. He and his father were happy. But still no friends. And Aunt D died in her sleep before she could see him graduate middle school. Melvin was devastated.

Her death drew him even further from the world around him. He gained an enormous amount of weight. His father understood why Aunt D's death hit him so hard, but he couldn't understand the ongoing depression his son endured. No matter how hard he'd try to get his boy to join an after-school program or take on a sport, Melvin was content with his alone time and seemed to prefer his own company.

He was pulled from an English class and summoned to the principal's office at the end of his sophomore year in high school. There, he was met with two officers, a social worker, and the school principal to bestow the earth-shattering news that his father had been killed on the job by a suspect robbing the department store at gunpoint.

Melvin's father had accumulated a very small pension at the department store. A moderate life insurance policy and the department store gave the surviving next of kin a tiny settlement. Melvin used the money to fund housing and board throughout his last years of high school. He morbidly moseyed his way through his final years of grade school education.

In the beginning, in the year following his father's murder, his classmates did what they could to provide condolence. Even the ones that didn't know him or notice him at all. Suddenly, people were smiling at him and waving as they walked by him in the hall. It was nice at first. He began noticing the pity in the eyes as they tried to keep a straight face to make him believe they cared. They were not told to be nice to him because some adult instructed them that it was the appropriate thing to do for those who'd lost the only family they'd ever known. He got sick of their pitiful eyes and started to mock their sympathetic glares with snap expressions in response. So, the whole school was repulsed or scared of him. They kept their distance, and that suited Melvin just fine.

His grades didn't suffer. He maintained his B- to C grade point average all the way up to graduation. He never took on an after-school activity. He never found a sport he liked. At the end of the school day, he was at home alone, reading up on serial killers, crime dramas, and any other hostility that tickled his interest.

A state-appointed representative was assigned to keep tabs on Melvin until he came of age. His name was Issac. He was in his late twenties and just graduated from college with a degree in social sciences. He got the job with the state through a job fair his alma mater sponsored on campus during his senior year. Issac had a thing for helping others find their way. Surprisingly enough, Melvin took to Issac quickly, and the two became fast friends. They would even hang out together socially as Issac pulled Melvin out of his dark shell and saw the world with fresh eyes.

Issac had a thing for murderous tales, too. They often sat up for hours discussing various serial killers and unsolved mysteries. They both spent endless time alone studying. For the first time in his life, Melvin felt comfortable enough to open up to someone and share his deeper wonderings, ponder his taboo interests, someone to talk to. Melvin was nearly ready to call it a friendship.

Graduation had come. Melvin had decided he wouldn't attend his graduation a week before and even months before. There was no one to graduate for. The principal would announce his name and no one would be there to cheer for him as he crossed the stage. The entire senior class may have already made a pact to go hush when his name was called — they hated him so much by then. It was how he preferred it, though. It was safer alone. There is less room for the hurt to creep into steel everything you're trying to hold on to.

"So hold on to nothing."

He said to himself while his father's coffin was lowered into the ground years before at his funeral.

But Issac had found a way inside his spirit and lifted it up every moment they spent together. And when Issac found out he planned to miss his big day, he wouldn't let that go down without a fight.

"That's crazy talk," Issac told Melvin over a six-pack of Cola and some nachos just a few weeks before graduation. "You've gotta walk the plank. You've earned it."

"No one's going to be there to see me —"

"You'll be there to see you, Mel," He got up from the chair and sat beside Melvin on the couch. He put his arm around his shoulder and tugged him in tight, to him. Trying to make eye contact. "Look at me, Mel."

He did.

"You're dad is looking down on you with that big broad smile you inherited from him and he's beaming with pride. He'll be there at that graduation to cheer you on, and the best thing is that you'll be the only one to hear it, and it's all yours. Only for your ears." He tugged at Melvin's shoulder, pulling him closer. "Your dad raised a very special man. I can see that. So what if they don't understand you? It's your day, too."

"Will you be there?"

Issac's hand seemed to leap from Melvin's shoulder at the request. He settled himself a little ways from Melvin but stayed on the couch. Melvin noticed a change in Issac as if he'd offended him. "I shouldn't have—"

"No," Issac said, looking down at the floor like he'd dropped something but found nothing to pick up. "I mean — Yes. I will do my best to be at your graduation. When is it? What time? I need to be sure I can make it, or I shouldn't promise you anything."

"It's alright, Isc," Melvin told him before looking at the floor for the item they couldn't find now. For a moment they both wonder what they'd lost between them just then. Or did they see something there that neither of them knew they wanted? "You don't have to come—"

"I'm going to be there," Issac confirmed. "I'll reschedule whatever I may have planned that day. But there's no sense in being in the audience to cheer you on as you trot across that stage if you're not going to hear it. Ok?"

Melvin's smile burst through those chubby cheeks like it was Christmas morning. "OK." He said as he stuck out a plump hand to shake.

Issac shook that fat hand hard enough for Melvin to know he could count on him to keep his word.

When Issac left him alone late that night, he thought about all the great talks they'd had and how close they'd become over the year Issac had been assisting him. Since his father's death, Melvin had begun to think himself cursed. How else could he explain to himself the sudden death of his mother during child bird. The immediate death of Aunt D. Ultimately leads his life to the untimely death of his father.

His only known relative. His lifeline. Melvin had drawn his spirit into the deepest emotional hole he could find and thought no one would be brave enough to pull him out of it.

Then came Issac with his familiarity. His humor. His companionship. What he thought he'd never have, Melvin finally began to believe possible in his cursed life. He said a prayer to his father that night. Thanking him for watching over him through his new friend. He thanked God that humanity had not forsaken him. No matter how hard he pushed it away.

The days ahead felt great. Melvin walked around the school with his head up and even spoke to some people he liked and knew they might like him too. Someone he didn't realize saluted him by name as he passed him in the hall on the exchange of classes. The last week of school was dreamlike for Melvin. He felt better than he ever had since his father told him how his mother died. His father cried in his arms that day. He could never lift the weight of that sadness.

Those last days of school brought about hope for a new beginning.

Strangely enough, it was already too late when he noticed that he hadn't heard from Issac all week. It was a Friday. The graduation was set to take place that Sunday afternoon on the rear lawn of the high school. Friday night came and went without a word from Issac. Melvin tried not to worry himself but couldn't help but think something was terribly wrong.

"It's not like him," he said to no one in the living room.

Maybe it was to his father. Maybe to the mother, he killed at birth. Maybe Aunt D.

"He would have called by now. Stopped by."

Just then, he realized that he knew no one in Issac's life that he could call to check up on him. Not a friend or mother or sibling or acquaintance. No father to call. No one. The panic started to rise in him.

"Something is wrong," he started telling himself as he paced his apartment, trying to find out why Issac hadn't called or stopped by. Then he began to think about the last time we were together. Issac's arm around his shoulder. The tug. His kind words. "Something is terribly wrong," he said.

You're right.

He finally heard the menacing, dark voice he dreaded he'd listen to again. The one he only thought he heard when Aunt D died. And again, when his father passed. Confirmation that the curse had not been lifted and spiritual proof that it did exist. This time the dread was clearer than it had been when he was called into the principal's office in middle school. The curse made itself known by speaking again.

Turn on the box. Check the news.

Hastily, he dashed into the living room. He snatched the remote from between the cushion of the plush black couch and aimed it at the forty-two-inch TV against the wall. It clicked on with a sharp flare. The channel was already tuned to the news, and there was a brief about the murder of a gay couple found dead on Miami Beach that morning. The police believe the couple were victims of a brutal attack spawned by an altercation around the couple's sexual orientation. The suspects were apprehended and are being sequestered for any information regarding the death of the couple. They identified the names of both men killed, but all Melvin could hear was the name of his near friend. The young, energetic man pulled him out of his dark space into a light he never thought possible to even see. And that light had been snuffed out by beach thugs who probably thought they were doing the country a favor.

I bet he put on a show. That's what got him in trouble.

"You stop that. Issac was a good man."

Who liked to show out with all those other good men. You know it ain't right. You saw the way he came on to you that night. Thinking he was fooling somebody with that daddy bullshit. He got the bashing he deserved.

"Can't show out anymore," Melvin said back to the voice that escaped his thoughts and entered the house. He held the remote in the direction of the TV and turned the newscast off.

They like to show their sex. Makes them feel in the power of it.

"He got what he deserved."

CHAPTER 14
CAUGHT OUT THERE

"What are you going to do, Robert? There's no way you'll be able to leave without her seeing you." Tessa's voice questioned through the speakerphone. "She's in the elevator now as we speak."

Robert, petrified, hunched over his desktop, leaning into the phone. His stomach churned in knots. He felt faint and dizzy. Raoul stood beside him behind the desk, staring at the phone, waiting for further instructions. He looked over at Robert.

"You gonna be alright, Bobbie," Raoul said, dismissingly stepping from behind the desk and walking to the door. "I'm going to bounce before she gets here. No sense in making matters worse. Right?"

"Rob. Something is wrong with Arlette." The speakerphone said.

"I can't talk about this right now, Tessa."

"But, wait, she's frea-" he slapped his finger over the receiver, cutting off the call.

Raoul was already on the other side of the door when the double doors of the center elevator car opened, and the lights inside flickered like strobes in a dance hall. Through the glass walls dividing the office section from the elevator bank, Robert could see his wife emerge from the dancing lights of the elevator box. She looked like a butterfly demonically transformed. Her morning work attire was ragged and torn and hung on her like old rags as if the sole survivor of an astronomic wreck, unbeaten and ready for more fight. Arlette stood like Lady Liberty, deprived of her torch, waiting for justice.

Raoul's back was to the window doors of the entrance to the elevator bank and he didn't see Arlette descend from the elevator. The horrified look on Robert's face made him turn around to find her standing at the entrance. He didn't seem to notice the ax dangling behind her right leg. Robert did, though. By the time he had, it was already too late.

The phone rang through the room again. Rob did not answer this time.

"Wow! Did she chop off all that gorgeous black hair?" Raoul asked. "Her stylist did a terrible job on that cut. Shesh!" He shook his head.

"What are you doing?" Robert yelled to him.

"Letting her in," Raoul said. "Looks like she forgot her access card. This is your problem now, Baby Bobbie. We probably shouldn't do this again."

He was at the entrance door and pushed the safety unlock button to let Arlette through.

The phone continued to ring loudly in Rob's office. The rain was pouring down and beating against the row of windows. A burst of lighting caressed the black sky as the thunder clapped, causing all three bodies in the office to start. Each looked to the sky.

Raoul pushed the right double glass door open. The phone rang on and on.

CHAPTER 15
STOP IT, JOSE!

"-freaking out in the elevator! Robert. She's got an ax! She's beating at the elevator car like a madwoman. Robert, you've got to get out of there now!" Tessa screamed into the receiver. She was panic-stricken watching her former friend and co-worker in an outraged tangent like a wild animal in a cage. There was something demonic in her old friend's elevator act. It was as if there were two sides of Arlette in a struggle to take possession of her body as she wheeled the brazen ax around the box, creating major damage to the car with the strength a woman her size shouldn't have. Her face was distorted into shapes and mugs of vast variety when she finally raised up one hand with the long braid twisted in her hand above her head. She swiftly sliced through the ragged braid, separating it from the top of her head with one swipe. The blade slightly nicked her inner bicep, opening a visibly bloody wound.

Tessa gasped loudly, waking herself from the horrifying vision. She saw Jose laughing horse, heaving gags at the screen and noticed he was still streaming the video live online. She swats him over the head with an open hand. "What the hell is wrong with you?" She yelled. "Take that

163

video down and do your job. She has an ax. She's freaking out in the elevator. What is your problem?"

"Don't blame me," Jose said, turning to her. "The guard in the lobby let her in looking like that. It ain't my business what she does."

"Jose, you need to call the police. This is serious."

"She ain't gonna do nothing."

"Look at her!"

"She's gonna have to pay for the damage to the elevator. That's on her."

Tessa tried calming her voice to get through to him, "Jose, stop with the video streaming. This is real life. And she's about to commit a crime. You need to call the police."

"She ain't that crazy."

"You don't know that," Tessa said. She picked up the receiver of the security office phone. "I'm calling Robert's extension again." She said, staring down at the screen with Arlette in the elevator.

The lights were flickering. There was broken glass scattered all around Arlette, who had fallen to the floor of the damaged box and sobbed in great heaves. When she lifted her face to the camera's view, the agony in it manifested the tortured soul deep inside her. Broadening those distorted formations Tessa had seen before. This had to be possession. Tessa's own face distorted as she watched the crippling overcome her co-worker. It frightened her.

The phone line rang unanswered. Tessa could see Robert standing over his desk on a monitor near Arlette's elevator monitor; Raoul was leaving the room. Arlette got up from the elevator floor when the double doors opened, the lights on the screen dancing incessantly.

A large flash of white light seemed to blind all the screens for a fleeting moment before the pictures revealed themselves again. What they exposed made Tessa and Jose jump to attention.

"I better call the police," Jose finally decided.

"You think?" Tessa shook her head and narrowed her eyes.

Jose closed the phone line to Robert's office and dialed 911. Tessa clasped her cell phone to her chest as she listened to Jose and watched the security screens. Her jaw dropped wider. Her eyes strained open in helpless fear.

"Oh, my dear girl," she quietly said.

Chapter 16
ELEVATOR WEDDING BELLS RINGING

In the quiet, rumbling rise of the elevator car, Arlette muddled over the days before her secret marriage to Robert Hamilton. The elevator floor indicator bells like the church bells of time, sounding the hours' countdown to the final moment of the nuptials. There was endless bickering between the pending bride and groom about nothing important. Robert was jumpy at the mention of the big day; the wedding talk was met with fits that led to Robert leaving the condo and getting home just hours before work. She blamed it on cold feet. Robert feels bad because her father spared no expense in giving his baby girl the wedding of her dreams.

Spoiled bitch. He must have thought then. *Use that spoiled bitch.* The edges of her eyelids burned at the memory of those early days. The elevator bell dings.

He must have been lying to her about running late from work. She wanted to be mad at him for possibly exposing her to some type of sexual disease, but he hadn't touched her for sex since the first year of their marriage. Even then, it was sparing and unaffectionate. No matter how sexy she tried to become. Was he attracted to the money and the opportunity to shove a card in any head honcho's hand that was looking? The ambition was the genuine attraction. He was hungry for the gorgeous packaging. She could tailor his life to design with hers and make things fit when they didn't.

The elevator bell dinged.

It didn't even embarrass Robert that her father paid for everything down to the ring for both the bride and the groom. None of his family attended the wedding. Just college friends she barely saw him speak to on the phone or on social media. Her father threw his lavish expenses in Rob's face at the rehearsal dinner, and Robert didn't even flinch. He carelessly excused himself from the room and returned when the dinner was nearly over.

The elevator bell dinged.

They agreed to meet at the altar.

He had a bachelor party with his suspiciously giggly drunk college friends. At the same time, she went off to dinner with her stepmother and cousins she barely knew. The entire night, her stepmother hinted at how unfit she was for that cute white boy and how she'd never be able to keep him, that she was his black girl fetish he'd eventually outgrow. *Why hadn't any of his family come to the ceremony?* Her stepmother had whispered in Arlette's ear at the reception. *Have they got something against their daughter-in-law?* She remembered Emma slightly cackled at her own words.

The ax hummed heat into Arlette's back. The elevator bell dinged.

When the bridal party got her to the church on time, in a stunning white dress, her hair styled in a thick French braid decorated in white flowers and pearls under a modest veil that hung to her waist, she was met with looks of surprised admiration. They knew to expect a dazzling bride, but something in their faces seemed troubled as the wedding party ushered her into the church, and the guests followed her with their looming eyes down the aisle. As she got closer to her groom at the end, he was unshaven, and his tuxedo looked as if he'd partied and slept in it, barely arriving on time for his own wedding.

As he raised the vale to announce their vows, a rush of liquor, stale cigarettes, and male sex diffused her senses, nearly sending her into a rage at the altar. He casually smiled at her with something that looked like an apology. He shrugged his shoulders and giggled. There was no trace of a woman in that scent rising off him. She could smell Robert but did not recognize the other sent. She said her vows anyway. When he came in to kiss the bride, she pulled away before giving in. There was a small gasp and a sigh from the witnesses.

She pulled the black leather bag from her back, removed the ax, and tore away the store packaging until she met the shining silver blade. The elevator bell dinged.

That man's sex musk filled the walls of her memory in that tiny box of the elevator. Arlette broke into a vicious rage, banging the ax against the four walls of the small space as if in a whirlwind of a trance. She broke the glass covering the ceiling lights with a careless ax swing. The broken glass sprinkled down around her like thick raindrops. The lights flickered from exposure. Arlette beat dents into the elevator walls as she screamed obscenities and promised violence in what looked like a ceremonial dance before a sacrifice. Suddenly, her spine stiffened. She pulled the tattered ponytail braid taught against a balled fist, extended above her head, and with a vicious scream from her gut, she snapped the ax through her thick braid, severing it from the top of her head. She opened a wound in her arm.

Finally, she fell to her knees in the broken glass, re-opening the wounds in her legs. Creating new ones. She sobbed in heavy, exhausting heaves as she curled into a ball with the ax lying in front of her. Her hand extended inches from the handle's release. She could hear it laughing at her. Maybe even with her.

The elevator bell dinged again. And the doors opened to her floor. The sobbing fell away as she picked up the ax, completely impervious to her pain. She stepped out of the open door into the elevator bank.

When she first saw Robert over the phone behind his desk and Raoul walking from the office saying goodbye, the scene seemed just as innocent as another day at the office. They were co-workers hammering out a deal on a late night that ended in itchy eyes and redness. It seemed harmless on the surface.

It was Robert's crotch that gave it away. His fly was down and slightly opened, revealing his boxer briefs.

The entire act of sexual brutality returned to her like she was seeing the video on repeat. How her husband's Latin lover beat at his body as he thrust his pelvis into his backside. The ecstasy on her husband's face as the act went down across the desk she helped him earn. The disgrace, the dishonesty, the disgust voracious and rising. Raoul approached the glassed-in entrance after saying a few words to her husband she could not hear.

Raoul paused to examine Arlette's appearance. She didn't care what he thought. And he didn't seem to recognize the ax dangling from her hand. Probably mistaking it for a handbag. He looked at her and smiled again. Arlette tucked the ax a bit further behind her right leg. The blade scraped a new cut on the back of her leg. Another she couldn't feel. The icy tickle of fresh blood streamed from the wound, and it seemed the blade of the ax fed from it as it scraped.

She smiled a hard, tight smile back at Raoul as he pressed the release button, opening the door.

"Getting an early start to the workday?" Raoul said as he pushed the right-side glass door open. A flash of white lightning from the menacing storm outside filled the office as Arlette raised the ax above her head, bringing down the blade across Raoul's broad chest, splitting him open as if he were a blood sausage. Raoul stumbled to the floor, his body holding the door open. Then he was finally down on the ground, and his body propped the door open, Arlette stepped over him and entered the office. She heard Robert's screams. But it was too late to protest. It was time to pay the piper for all the lies told.

She hoped, for his sake, he was ready to pay as she raised the ax, locking glare with her helpless prey in his fishbowl fantasy. Arlette buried the ax in Raoul's vulnerable back.

She could hear Robert gasp in complete horror. The petrified look in his eye started a smile growing on her face.

CHAPTER 17
LETTIE'S STORM

Wide-eyed, his body quivering as if the office were ten degrees below zero, terror-stricken, Robert Hamilton watched his deranged wife bury the hatchet into Raoul's back after slashing his chest wide open. Manny's motionless body lay at the bottom of the glass door, propping it open like a doorstop.

Am I in a nightmare? Rob thought.

Arlette snatched the bloody axe blade from her victim's back and turned to the glass wall of Robert's office. Rob stood there in paralyzed disbelief. Trying to understand how his once self-contained wife had such a ruthless beast living just below the surface of her bitchy facade. She was behaving like a wild huntress on a mad killing spree to avenge a dying dream.

Moving quickly up the short aisle leading to Robert's office, Arlette was in the room before he could take a step from behind the desk. She bolted toward him. Raising the ax above her head and with a merciless swing, she brought it down into the ebony desktop, burying the blade in the faux wood surface. The weapon stood between them in a crack created by the force of impact. Arlette did not loosen her grip on the handle. Instead, she climbed on top of the desk like a gigantic spider. Robert fell back into his executive chair, surrendering to his fate. Arlette was a woman scorned, and she would have her revenge.

She kneeled, got right into his face, and sniffed him hard up and down his torso. The shape of her was wiry like a pretzel as she balanced her body on the desk, clinging to the handle of the ax buried in the desk. She tugged at the weapon, trying to release it from its trap.

"Fooled me once, Robert." She said. His eyelids stretched back, and the balls bulged from the sockets. "Fooled me twice." He flinched as she raised a long, black finger to his face. The nail was chipped and partially broken but was colored a dark red like blood. "Fool me again, and that wouldn't be very nice." She said in a sing-song tone that was haunting and miserable to Robert's ears.

Robert couldn't move under the glare of Arlette's threatening eyes. The creature on top of his desk had the body and face of his wife, but she was not his Lettie. The bloodshot, brooding eyes in the deformed features couldn't be the woman he once knew that stood stern under any pressure. Where had she gone? What had she become if this was her? "I caught you, Robert. No need to tell any more lies."

"What are you talking about?" Robert pleaded. "What are you doing here? What's wrong with you? Why did you slit Raoul open like a blood sausage?"

"He's an abomination! The both of you are. A sickness!" She screamed in his face. "I'm going to put an end to your lies once and for all, Robert J. Hamilton."

Robert's eyes widened in terror. Arlette yanked hard at the ax but couldn't pull it free from its mark on the desk. It stalled her anger as well. This gave Rob just enough time to run out of his office into the mass office space.

At the end of the aisle, he spot Raoul's still body wedged between the double doors. His back was soaked in blood. Rob thought he should check on him, but when he looked back into the office, he saw Arlette give a wrenching yank at the ax handle, setting it free. She raised it above her head and shot a sharp look at Robert. The rage had consumed her. She had transformed into a beast of rage. Her silky black hair was short, sweat-soaked, and wild about her head. The muscles in her legs and arms bulged from strain, making her look like a demonic statue.

Suddenly, a burst of lightning slammed into the large bay window, crashing into the glass and sending tiny shards scattered through the air of the office.

The glass wall opposite the window did not crash and protected Rob from the blast that blew up his office. But he saw his wife's body lacerated by the tiny shards that blew in with the wind and rain. The thunderclap that slammed the downtown area was powerful enough to shake the tip of the peninsula where their building stood. It knocked Arlette off the desktop where she tumbled to the floor. She was cut up and bloody all over. She rolled into a corner where she lay still. Her eyes were closed. Yet she maintained a tight grip on the ax handle, now free from the faux ebony desk.

Rob ran toward the elevator bank. Stepping carefully over Raoul's body. Frantically, he pressed the call button for the elevator. The center car Arlette had vandalized opened. Its flickering lights flash like signals. He peered inside to find the beaten car littered with broken glass and the wall dented and scared.

"No," Robert said, shaking his head in disbelief. It took him a moment to see that the scratches in the back wall of the elevator formed words that read: *rot in hell*, with wild markings like tiger or bear claws scattered around the words. His jaw dropped. He didn't want to risk getting inside, but when he looked to his office, Arlette was on her feet again with the ax erect in her hand. She exited the office, moving toward the elevator bank.

Rob ran to catch the car before it closed, but was too late. The elevator doors slammed on Robert, and Arlette stood over Raoul's body, threateningly facing him. "Where you gonna hide now, lover boy?" She said. Her eyes glimmered with wrath. Behind her in Rob's office, the rain poured in like waterfalls through the busted bay window. The storm looked like it was trying to get into the office for an appointment through the ready-made entrance. The storm seemed to fuel Arlette's rage. She lunged at Robert with a scream, raising the ax above her head.

As she made an impact, Robert was able to snatch the raised arm and wrestle her to the ground, paralyzing her wrist with the ax with a firm grip. He beat her hand against the floor until her grip on the handle loosed, and it fell to the floor. Robert jumped to his feet, turned from Arlette, and ran back into the office. Leaping over Raoul's body. Arlette screamed something that sounded like a tortured dog and grabbed the ax again. She got to her feet and took off behind Robert in a mad dash.

When the elevator bank went dead silent, Raoul opened his eyes, looking around to be sure he was alone. Seeing the coast clear, he worked his body into the bank, sliding along the floor, leaving a trail of blood behind him. Before he could get to the call button, the damaged center car doors opened. He examined the car in horror. "What the fuck?"

The vandalism didn't prevent him from crawling into the car, as the doors shut behind him once he was safely inside.

CHAPTER 18
CIGARETTES

"He's a pansy, Lettie. A fucking fruit cake," Mel said after a long inhale on his Newport 100. They were at their second smoke break on a Thursday afternoon just before the close of business for Arlette at The Chariot Mortgage group. Lettie just told Melvin about her engagement to Robert over the weekend wouldn't stop the stream of confessional joy spilling from her mouth between inhales and exhales of cigarette smoke. She went on about how happy she was over the engagement.

Melvin couldn't understand how she could be so overjoyed at the acceptance of a proposal she made. Her father provided the ring. Emma Silver arranged the meeting place for the proposal and practically begged Robert to accept when she warned him of Arlette's intentions.

Melvin held all this information because he'd been working in security for the last nine years and had grown close to several employees who like to take smoke breaks away from the crowds and longed for the company of a stranger to run on and on about their troubles, personal affairs. He'd had access to this nuptial drama from its festering beginnings through Amos Silver's wife, Emma. It grew when Arlette was in the thick of her success with the company and developed an insatiable desire for the smoke break. A cigarette. She forbade herself to stop at the many bodegas around the office to pick up her very own pack. Then, she'd have to label herself a smoker. That was frowned on across the board with the staff and especially with the executives. That habit had migrated to building's 'Help.' The sentiment wasn't policy, but those who indulged were encouraged to quit. As well they should be.

A very stressed and exhausted Arlette stepped out of the elevator into the lobby of One Liberty Plaza, away from the stress of a quickly rising Chariot Mortgage Group and all its demands that came with the rising success. The accounts won monthly. The search for new rewards. The time it took away from any bond she could make with anyone. A time before meeting Robert or even thinking about a New Hire Job Fair at the Jacob Javits Center.

The Rise.

Melvin spot Arlette minutes after departing from her stepmother, Emma. Emma stopped by the office to meet with some of the mortgage banking executives. She'd been Amos Silver's assistant for as long as Melvin had been on the job at Liberty Plaza. Nine years to the day when he saw Arlette and read by the language in her body standing in the center of the elevator bank. She looked lost as she glared from the left side exit to the right side. Melvin knew she was working for the mortgage company. Amos introduced him to his daughter with a proud face when she started her internship with the growing group.

The nine years between that time and then seemed to have sped by Melvin's eyes like a slide show as he watched her ponder. She was just a young, bright lady then. Finding her way, he could tell by how she shook his hand and looked him square in the eye the day they first met that she was all about business. Arlette was a stunning woman to admire. Her beauty came second to the determination behind those brown eyes. The workings of a woman out to prove to herself that she made her own way. Amos may have introduced her to Chariot Mortgage, but that determination earned her the positions she acquired.

Melvin saw that rise in her. He'd hear about Arlette through Amos' occasional visits to the office. Amos' wife, Emma, made it a habit to bum-a-smoke from her security guard smoke buddy.

Melvin wasn't really a smoker. Not regularly, anyway. He'd picked up the habit when he migrated to New York after the death of what would have been his first friend, Isaac. It was the only way he could stop thinking about him. Blaming his curse for Isaac's death. He sought employment in security like his father. Upon his search, he landed a job with a security company in New York. They were willing to train and help him get certified to carry arms. That job led to a permanent position at One Liberty Plaza, sneaking smoke breaks with executives, pretending they were his friends. Pretending they wanted more than the smoke, they bummed off him. In his eighteen years with the company as a security guard with One Liberty he had garnered enough gossip to fill a novel.

In Arlette beautifully standing between six elevator entrances looking like a lost little girl — probably for the first time in her life — he could tell that all she needed was someone to show her a way out.

"Arlette!"

She turned to face the person calling out her name from what seemed like a million miles away.

When her deep brown eyes set their stare on his face, and the huge bright smile grew beneath them, he blushed at being the cause. She seemed to remember him after all those years when Amos introduced them. Yes, she'd passed him every day in the lobby since then, but that was all she did. Pass him by. Not a hello. Not a single glance. And that day he gets a full-out smile as she advances to him.

"Melvin," She says through an exhausted breath. "You have no idea how good it is to see you right now."

Knowing full well that she, too, was not a smoker. Not yet, anyway. The idea of becoming one probably repulsed her. Melvin proposes, "Smoke?"

"Yes."

Arlette's confessional began that day and continued for nearly a year as their little secret. One smoke just before lunch on the basement level loading dock, tucked quietly in a corner by a door leading to a ramp that exit to the street. Then that quickly turned to a second smoke before the start of overtime, after take-out at her desk. Arlette was diligent in finding her smoke buddy in the lobby at his post as if waiting for her to arrive in that bank of quiet elevators.

Melvin was always available and had her brand ready — Newports — in the inside pocket of his duty jacket.

Mel — as Lettie began to call him when he mocked her father's nickname to her during one of their breaks together — was met that day forward with her broad, bright smile and anxious eyes. And greeted back with his greatest grin. Once he noticed these meetings would become a new and wanted cycle in his work day, he let his heart take over his mind, and he'd dream about her mostly when she wasn't around. Sweet dreams of kisses, fondling, and gropes he could only imagine. He would never bring himself to act on his desire. However, Arlette was kind to him. She didn't seem to mind his overweight or that he was, at least, seven or eight years her senior and — in his mind — way out of her league. When he dreamed of her it wasn't him he'd find in his dreams with her. It was another man. The handsome, in-shape, well-groomed, and financially stable version of himself. Wavy black hair, an adoring baby face, and a body that didn't repulse her to hold on to in the middle of the night. Not the fat, balding Ogar inhaling cigarette smoke with her during those breaks.

The shock was clearly visible when the opportunity came to show her a version of his better self — as clean as he could get it.

"We should get together after we both clock out tonight, Mel."

"What —" Melvin said through a choke on his last exhale. They were sharing a smoke. Arlette was making another failed attempt at quitting that day when she finally stopped at the bodega to pick up a pack before another stress full day at Chariot. She pounded the pack off to Melvin before they started on the cigarette they shared from the pack.

"Was it wrong of me to ask that?"

"No!"

"I just thought we'd have more time to chill and really get to know one another before I just abandon our time together. I am going to miss this."

"Me too." *If it ever really happens.* Melvin thought as he watched her lips take a smooth drag from the tan filter. The cherry glow at the other end of the white stick flickered a reflection in her brown eyes, making them sparkle.

"It's a stupid idea. I'm sorry I brought it up."

"I'd like to go out after work with you, Arlette." He waited, then asked, "Tonight is good for you?"

"It is."

And just like that, Melvin didn't have to pretend any longer. A door had been opened to reveal an opportunity to let someone in. She wanted to get to know him. What the hell could that mean? He pondered over the last five hours of the workday. He was glad he'd brought a full suite of clean civilian clothes with him to work. And the attire was evening-appropriate. It's black and hide the fat some. He continued to ponder as he looked up at the large clock behind him overhead. It was a dial display that looked as if the parts of the clock were embedded into the wall. It read six-ten.

Arlette would make her way down to the lobby to meet him no later than six-thirty. He wanted to be ready and waiting outside.

Others shouldn't see them together in case things didn't go as planned.

"Better we meet outside the building." He left his post without saying goodnight to the other guards. That was typical of any other work day. He hadn't made a single person there he wanted to say goodnight to until he met Arlette. And at her request, their hours together had been extended.

"I'll meet her at the entrance." He told himself aloud.

"Meet who?" Came the voice of the nosey rookie working the night shift. His name was Jose, Melvin remembered. He thought he was alone. He closed his locker and found Jose standing behind its door closing his pants to his uniform. Melvin scrunched up his face in disgust and looked the other way. "You got a hot date tonight, captain?" Melvin trained Jose, and the boy got a little too close with the nicknaming. Melvin grunt it off then as he got to know the new hire. He then let it stick when training was done and shifts unaligned their work hours.

"Your mama never warned you to stay out of grown folks business, private?" Was his dig back at his trainee.

"Yo. Chill, esse. I was just making small talk with a co-worker."

"Well, mind your own business, Rookie, and keep your eyes on the ball." Mel roared at Jose before he exited the locker room.

"I thought you had stood me up." Arlette said, exiting the entrance of the building to find Melvin waiting at the end of the short walkway. "You weren't at your station."

"I thought you'd want to meet outside the building."

"Discretion. I've always liked that about you, Mel." She said as a gentle smile opened her face to him. "Always looking out."

"Shall we?"

What surprised Mel as the night began was that Arlette was fine with walking the peers and chomping down on a hot dog while they sipped bag-covered forty ounces of Old English. She talked about her father like he was the king of industry and her desire to top his success just to show him up. She told him the truth about Emma's cruelty to her as she grew into a woman.

Mel pretended he didn't know who Emma Silver was, and Arlette gave no sign that he would know her stepmother at all. The gossip was too salacious to resist. She confessed that she knew her father was a womanizing cheat and had been unfaithful to his second wife for many years. She told him she knew that Emma only married her father for his money and to latch on to his success.

By the time she'd finished her story, they were atop a small man-made grassy hill, looking at the night lights of New Jersey float over the Hudson River. They'd done away with the hot dogs before sitting down. Arlette's forty of Old English was down to the last sip. They were half smoked out of the Newport she bought that morning and gave to him earlier that night. She'd taken the bottle out of the bag and used it to emphasize her points as she talked to Mel. His forty was half full. His eyes were hungry for more gossip while his lust for her lingered under the air between them.

Then, suddenly, the conversation stopped. They sat quietly on the grassy mound, staring into the reflected lights in the water of the Jersey shore. The night world around them had fallen so silent that they could faintly hear the noise of a party of people from the closing restaurant behind them.

"I'm sorry," Arlette finally said. "I'm sure you didn't expect to spend your evening listening to my sad story."

"It could have been worse."

"How?"

"I could be telling you mine."

His grin widened, and for the moment, Mel thought Arlette could see him. The version of himself he saw in his daydreams about his work friend's daughter. The handsome, toned and debonair Melvin his father always told him he'd become when he was a man. And even though his father's prediction never came to pass, in that fleeting moment on the grassy hill, he thought Arlette could see him.

She smiled back at him. Her eyes glazed over. Her expression could easily be mistaken for lust — even desire. Her upper body began to swirl with the sound of the waves in the river below. Still smiling back at Mel. Feeling the effects of the forty-ounce taking over, she leaned her face closer to Mel's when he tried to break their gaze.

Her movement caught him off guard, but he was ready to receive her. And though he'd never kissed or made out with a woman before — there had been escorts and prostitutes, but they were quick to get him off and collect the moment they saw him at the door — his fantasies had prepared him for the moment.

He let her black lips fall to his supple tan pair and was careful not to open his mouth or invite his tongue until she gave the signal. And when she opened her mouth to encase his lips in her warmth, Mel let loose his tongue and imagined he was the version of himself in his day dreams.

She kissed back.

He grabbed the back of her head to pull her face closer to his own.

She didn't care what her hair looked like or how it might feel. She kissed back. Then his free hand was around her waist and firmly pulling her into him. She came up for air. He buried his head into the cradle of her firm breast to sigh into the scent of her. She smelled like lilies and strawberries. Beer and cigarettes.

His heavy hands began to kneed her middle like she was clay in a sculpture's hands. She closed her eyes to allow herself the freedom to feel his hard touch. She let him kiss her clothed breasts. She allowed him the opportunity to taste what he desired and thought he'd never get.

He took her down onto the grass and topped her small body with some of the heavy weight of his own. He returned to her black lips for another taste and was met with lips tight as a fist.

"Get off me, Melvin."7

He didn't bother to respond. His gropes pressed harder against her breast. She tried to pull back. His grip was like a vice. His brow began to sweat.

"No!" She screamed. She slapped his face as hard as she could with her free hand. He laughed at her strike. Pinned her hand to the ground above her head and spit in her face.

"You're going to get it now, Fake bitch!"

The weight of him felt like nothing she could try to move. He would need to get off her if he were going to do anything. That's when she'd strike. She knew he was too chickenshit to kill her with his bare hands. He was horney. She was drunk. Thankfully, she came to her senses before she did something she'd regret for the rest of her life.

"You're not even hard, Mel," she casually said. "You gonna be able to get it up?"

"You fake bitch!" He raised his fat hand high to smack but stopped mid-air when he heard a voice cry out behind them.

"HEY!" It said.

Mel was quickly on his feet, uncovering Arlette. She stumbled to her feet and began descending the grassy hill.

CHAPTER 19
FACES OFF

"Come out and face me like a man, you coward!" Arlette screeched in the dark air of the large office space. Methodically, she marched down the aisles in the blackness. She knew the layout of the space well enough to see through the hazy dim of the exit signs and emergency spotlights glowing in the ceiling. There was no dark outline of Robert's broad-shouldered frame to sneak up on or surprise. She stopped in the center of an aisle to listen.

The stormy winds outside raged at the bay windows surrounding the office space. A wall of rain cascades the glass, making the space look like it was in a car wash. The rain is so heavy it up-struck the view of the neighboring buildings. Rain torrents flow through the broken window of Rob's office like a ruptured dam. The rain soaked the floor.

She passed his office twice in her frantic search through the dark. *He would try to call the police.* She thought. That didn't matter. He'd be dead before they got to the lobby. Robert would meet his fate tonight for his betrayal and embarrassment at their marriage.

189

The tip of the ax blade shimmered against an emergency sign light as Arlette raised the weapon above her head, anticipating Robert attempting to be brave in the darkness. She wanted to be ready for him should he decide to charge at her. There was still no sign of him in the massive space of cubicles. The blade agreed with her. Robert would have to meet his end on this night. This was more than a lie. More than a broken dream. He had broken any trust left between them with his secret desires.

"This office is made of glass, heathen!" She shouted. She was outside his office in the aisle between his door and the start of the work cubes. The rain hissed behind her. "Everyone can see what everyone else is doing; even when you think they aren't looking, they see. Spying on you. Looking over your shoulder. Getting all up in your business. What do you think they will say about me tomorrow in the break room, Robert!?" Her voice was high-pitched and cracking. "If a man also lies with a man as he lieth with a woman, both of them have committed an abomination. They shall surely be put to death; their blood shall be upon them."

Rob couldn't figure out where the bible verse came from. Arlette had never been a religious woman before. The last time they were even at a church was their wedding day and before that, she would always speak negatively toward any religious practice. *Why the sudden change in faith?* He thought, crouched down beneath a cubical near to where Arlette stood shouting over him. He was quiet enough not to be noticed over the chatter of the pouring rain and his wife's screaming. Arlette didn't sound like herself either. Her voice was husky, deeper, manlike.

Rob pulled a phone down from the desk he was hiding under and had the receiver pressed hard against his chest. He had not dialed the police yet. He was afraid she would hear the dial tone or even the operator when the call was finally answered. He planned to quickly dial the police and then make a beeline for the staircase that was only a few cubicles away from his hiding place. He couldn't move now. He'd surely be caught. He could outrun Arlette any day of the week, but she was too close now. He was right under her nose and still unnoticed. Rob held his breath tight under the pressure.

"Come out, abomination!" She howled in that sinister, unfamiliar voice. "The time for atonement has come upon you, Sinner. Your blood shall be upon you!" The scream was a spine-curdling whale of heinous sound. It sounded as if it came from everywhere in the space and mixed with the rhythm of the thunderous storm outside. *Why had the police not arrived after the window broke out?* Rob thought. *Where was security?* He heard a sudden crash of glass and metal.

When he peered over the desk where he was hiding and looked through the glass partition framed in white painted metal, he saw his wife on a destructive rampage, destroying a cubical three rows down from where he hid. She was like a wild beast slinging the ax about uncontrolled and colliding with whatever was in the line of fire. She had clearly lost her mind, grunting and groveling at the cubicle as she wheeled the ax. But she was far enough away for Rob to make a run for the stairwell. He thought he would have to abandon the idea of calling the police until he had a second thought.

Quickly crouching down under the cubicle again with the office phone, he opened the line and dialed nine eleven. Strangely enough, the line rang repeatedly unanswered. He lay the phone down with the call still ringing in, putting it on speaker so that the ringing could be heard through the space. Then he steadfastly crawled from the cube, staying low enough out of view until he was at the staircase.

Arlette finally heard the ringing of the speakerphone and stopped her violent rant to listen to where the call was coming from. An operator finally answered the open line.

"Nine one one. What's the address of your emergency?" Said the friendly but concerned voice through the speakerphone. Arlette stood over the phone, now angered at the fact that Robert was right under her chin and she didn't smell him. "Hello?" The operator's voice asked when there was no reply. Arlette screamed a vicious cry as she raised the ax above her head and brought it down on the phone, breaking it into pieces on impact. Somehow, it was still in operation.

"Hello!" the operator said, more anxiously this time. "Where are you located? I can send help." Arlette beat the phone into silence. Then she looked up and saw the horror-stricken face of her husband standing by the staircase exit door. He looked as if he were in the devil's presence, standing there petrified by what he had witnessed. *She killed the phone.* Arlette smiled at his feeble disposition. It was entertaining to see Robert frazzled. He had a way of always keeping his cool that now, when threatened with black violence, changed to white panic and pure shame. She could see through the dimly lit space that he felt responsible for her maddening outburst. He wanted to apologize for bringing it out. But it was too late for sorry. The damage was done. She was damaged goods in search of vengeance.

Rob pushed the door open to the staircase, quickly stepping inside. Arlette abandoned her phone torture and ran off after him.

He was only a few flights down from the fifty-fifth floor when he heard the door slam above him. He thought he could hear Arlette's panted breathing like a wild boar on the hunt. He quickened his descent down the narrow and winding staircase, never a moment's pause on a platform to catch his breath.

Arlette was two floors above him but gaining quickly. Robert could hear her footfalls, her panting and sobs, and occasionally, he would hear the metal blade of the ax slam against the metal railings of the stairwell. The sound would bounce off the walls of the stairwell like a church bell at high noon. Rob knew there was no point in trying to talk to Arlette or be rational. She was too far gone for that. But he wondered how she found out. Her reaction was no surprise. However, he never suspected she would go so far as to try to butcher him.

Robert paused a moment, getting the idea to stop the foolish chase, overpowering his wife and somehow breaking her free from the weapon. A second thought popped into his consciousness: the memory of Arlette standing over his desktop vigorously, trying to free the embedded ax from the tabletop. The power that seemed to possess her was inhuman, barbarous, and vicious. He would be no match for the hell it would unleash on him. He took off running down the steps again, quickening his feet, an attempt at being sure-foot descending two steps at a time, occasionally chancing three steps in a long stride as he could hear Arlette's footfalls gaining on him. The chiming of the ax beating the metal railing was like a warning bell. *Where were the police? Why had security not come?*

Maintaining his fair lead on the way down the stairwell, Robert took a four-tier leap and missed stepping, losing his balance. He came down hard on a twisted ankle as he lunged forward, head first down a flight of steps. At the platform below the steps, the right side of his face smacked the wall, knocking him out for a moment while his body fell to the platform floor. He could hear Arlette's footfalls getting closer as he floated in and out of consciousness lying there helpless. He knew he should move, but his ankle throbbed with pain, and his head felt larger than a globe.

The church bell gonging of the ax sailed through the cavernous well, reminding Rob of that morning before his wedding ceremony and how he woke up drunk in the bed with all his college brothers around him, their clothes disheveled, some of them undressed. He remembered the night of sex and how good it felt to have that last dance before the church bells chimed in the lie he'd have to live for the rest of his life. This moment surely wasn't in the plan. Had it been, he would have made the other choice, to love his brothers openly and stave off the common life. Shave the beard and love the man beneath it. Instead, he pulled up his man musk-laced tuxedo, woke the boys, and got them dressed properly while he had a liquid breakfast to face the day ahead.

The church bell gong of the ax against the railing chimed in even closer and sounded more intentional than before, deliberate with defiance and stubborn with a vengeance.

Then there she stood, on the platform above the one he had fallen to. Her footfalls came to a halting stance before beginning again when she saw the broken body of her husband at the foot of the landing. She took a sure, smooth slide down the stairwell to meet Robert on his back and wounded.

He felt like he was looking up from his grave as his wife stood above him, looming down at him like the vulture she seemed to have changed into. In the dim light of the stairwell and the daze of his face crashing against the wall, Arlette seemed like a deformed shadow in a sick dream. Her marble-black skin is shiny from sweat and rain. Her anger seemed to be the cause of the rumbling of the raging storm around them. His head pounded with the remembered rhythm of the ax-banging church bells down the stairwell. He drifted in and out of consciousness only to return, and she was closer. A hardened statue of Aphrodite, with Nephritis's brow and Mona Lisa's maddening grin against a hazed canvas. She was motionless, standing between his spread legs like a viper. The ax blade twinkled in the dim light of the stairwell. It seemed to draw the light to it so that it could dance around in Robert's thoughts.

"Arlette. You don't want to do this. Whatever this is, you don't want to do this-"

"You're a sickness." She hissed. She was calm. He was trapped. "I can smell it on you. I always could. I didn't want to recognize the scent, so I masked it from my own nose. I ignored the stench and lived around it. But it was always there, Robert-"

"You're not making sense…"

"I made up all sorts of excuses, but I knew the truth all along. I just didn't want to believe you would do this to me."

"What did I do? I didn't do anything, Arlette. Talk to me. What are they telling you?"

"I saw you with my own two eyes." The ax was active in her hand again. Blade even with her waist. "Don't lie to me, Robert!"

Robert braced himself further against the wall, readying for the pending attack. The pain in his ankle sent shouting agony up his leg into his back, then up his spine, into his brain, where it throbbed with a hot pounding. He knew the bone was broken. His fate was clear to him.

"I should split you right down the middle." She told him. Then, without a moment's hesitation, something seemed to cease her, even by her own surprise, as she grasped the ax with both hands and raised it high above her head. Robert looked up into her shocked face as it looked like she was pleading with him to help her. But what could he do?

"Lettie, don't!" Robert commanded. He had come back to himself fully and, for a moment, felt a burst of strength empower him. He raised both hands up over his face as if they would protect him, and with his good leg, he kicked out. His foot slammed against Arlette's calve hard enough to cause a snapping noise and throw her off balance. She stumbles backward, tumbling over the railing and out of sight.

Robert quickly managed to crawl to the edge of the platform to look over the edge into the deep well. He had not heard a scream or crash or any sign that the body had hit any surface on the way down. All he knew was that she had fallen over. And when he looked over the edge, he found his wife there. Dangling from her unyielding grip on the blue ax handle. The blade caught the edge of the landing, bracing her fall. But the grip was unsteady, and Arlette was making no stride to help herself.

"Arlette. Baby, reach for my hand. Baby, please. Arlette, reach for me." He reached down with his arm fully extended for her to safely grab, and she did as he commanded without struggle. There was no care in her eyes. Her grip was feeble like she was on a walk in the park instead of trying to save her own life. He gripped her arm firmly in his hand. She let the ax slide off the ledge. He could barely support her weight now.

She felt light as a feather. Free as a bird in flight.

"You need to climb up, honey. I can't hold you much longer." Rob said, panting hard. He was right. His grip was already slipping. Arlette must have sensed that and looked up at him. She saw the man she married in the ice-blue eyes of his tanned face. Saw the man she thought had loved her and wanted to protect her from the evils of the world in their garden in the sky. The man she thought she had married. He was masculine, heroic, successful, charming, and easy on the eyes. But that was all lies. A ruse to cover up his sin. And for that, he could not live.

She wheeled the ax hard above her, burying it in the center of Robert's forehead. His mouth gagged open at impact as his grip on his wife loosed, and she blissfully melted into the dark of the stairwell until there was a hard-hollow thud that sounded through a cavernous space.

The ax lay embedded in Robert's skull, sucking his blood like a vampire. He finally tilted his lifeless head in death's defeat as the blade slipped from the scar, falling down the well in a tumble, sounding like a church's bell as it banged against the metal railings out of time in its decent.

When it reached the bottom, it landed just above the lifeless hand of Arlette's broken body in the pool of blood beneath it. Arlette stares up into the stairwell at the silhouette of her husband's dead body dangling from what must be the twentieth-floor platform.

There's a victorious grimace opening her face.

CHAPTER 20

CODA

Raoul was found barely alive, slumped over. His back smooshed against the back wall under the scratched message from Arlette's elevator rampage. At three thirty A.M., the police arrived and discovered him just as the elevator car dropped into the lobby bank and opened before anyone had called for it. Security had finally put in a call about the domestic disturbance in the office space where there was a weapon involved. The head of the mortgage company branch, who nearly fired Arlette that morning, and nine other managers within traveling distance were called to the scene for questioning.

Amos and Emma Silver were called to the scene.

At first, the officer could not find the culprit involved in the vandalism. It was suspected that some young people had broken into the building and decided to horse around in an empty office during a storm. But the shattered glass, the ax imprint in the desk, the blood-stained walkways, and the half-dead body leaned more towards something deliberately nefarious.

199

Jose tried to convince Tessa to go home and make it like she was never there, but she wouldn't have that. Tessa confessed the story to the police and forced Jose to show them the video. In doing this, they had to admit their part in the matter. Tessa was more ready to face those consequences than Jose. She didn't feel she had done anything wrong. Arlette had a right to know what her husband was doing behind her back. Her life was at stake. She never suspected it would end like this.

The damage to the office was meticulous but significant enough to warrant closure for at least a month. This would slow down business and hinder the bottom line at the end of the year numbers. It would be safer to close the office space and eat the financial loss on the lease.

Jose and Tessa did not have access to the footage in the stairwell. So they did not see where Arlette and Rob ran off to once the commotion happened in the main view of the security camera. But security in the lobby had full access.

When they were directed back downstairs to Melvin Rodriguez, he was gone from his post and could not be found anywhere in the building. When the authorities tried to see him at his known address, they discovered he had never lived there. Melvin Rodriguez didn't exist in any database under the provided credentials and didn't seem to exist at all, though he had been on the building security payroll for nine years.

He left the video of the episode in the stairwell between Rob and Lettie on replay before leaving his station. Tessa, Jose, and the officers watched with shocked faces as the incident played out repeatedly over the monitor. The bodies were recovered and collected once the paramedics arrived.

Arlette was found in a pool of blood so vast it coated the floor at the bottom of the deep fall. Not far from her hand, the ax was later confiscated for evidence.

Rob's body was found twenty flights above on a stairwell platform. Lifeless, leaning over the edge as if he were trying to catch something that caught him instead. His face split in two at the center like a splayed pant fly.

Raoul was rushed to the hospital. He had surgery to mend his chest and his open back. The doctors found him lucky to be alive, and his body mass was probably why the injuries didn't cut so deep. He came clean to the officers about his affair with Robert that night. He told them it was mutual and consensual, despite what it may have looked like on the video they had confiscated as more evidence. When they asked him about Melvin Rodriguez, he could not give them any more information than they had already obtained. Like everyone else, he had seen Melvin around but found the now phantom security guard peculiar and nosey.

The police brought up the incident between Raoul and me in the copy room to him and how Melvin broke that up. Raoul denied it ever happened. The police didn't question him further about it. He went on to heal and got a settlement from the company to keep his mouth shut to the public about what went down that night. And he was to find another job. Both of which he did and was never heard from again.

The company relocated to an office across the Hudson in Jersey City on the harborside. The excuse to the employees was that the company was rebranding and thought a new space would boost the morale in the change. Many employees of Chariot Mortgage stayed with the company after signing a waiver, promising never to engage in personal sexual relations with a colleague in their branch or any other location within the organization. Despite this signing, many employees still engage in relations among co-workers. Some have since been caught and inconspicuously asked to leave. Others have been far craftier in their after-work activities.

Tessa was not dismissed from her duties as manager of her team. Instead, she was promoted to a larger team once the divisions were merged and staff tightened. The company commended her on her full cooperation with the police and thanked her for exposing a scandal that could easily have gotten out had it gone unnoticed. She had to let go of Jose. It wasn't the most significant loss as she realized how much of a coward he was that night of the incident. Any man who would record and exploit anyone for humiliation didn't deserve to be loved. She was happy to relinquish her duties to him that night. He was arrested at the scene for aiding and abetting a crime. He would stand trial, and Tessa had agreed to testify against him.

The search for Melvin Rodriguez continued for months while the prosecution built its case against Jose. The story died down in the media along with all the other storm stories that came about that fatal night in the financial district. There were incidents of record-high violence during that storm, as if the whole of Manhattan had a momentary lapse of rational and went mad for a moment in fits of anger. For Tessa, the incident haunts her thoughts constantly and invades her sleep often.

One early spring morning, while on her way to work in Jersey City through the bowels of the subway on Fulton and Broadway. Tessa exited the four-train exit at Liberty Place in Manhattan and entered the One Liberty Place building lobby where Chariot Mortgage Company once was.

She arrived at the security turnstile before she realized her mistake as she released her badge from her purse.

"Ms. Hernandez?" She heard a male voice question. "I believe you are in the wrong building."

Horror ceased her throat as she looked up to find Melvin Rodriguez standing next to her at the turnstile. His chubby hand stretched out to stop her from crossing. She stepped back from him as if he were a killer. Instead, she saw something vicious and red in his eyes that flashed there for a long moment, then was gone again. She gasped.

"You used to work here." He said. "With the girl who killed her husband. A catastrophic incident, wasn't it? I heard you saw the whole thing on the security video -- with the police."

Tessa didn't know what to say and could only stand facing him with her eyes wide and her body like stone. Where had he come from? Had he talked to the police? She was too afraid to ask anything. She could only slowly back away from him into the crowded lobby.

"Yes." She sighed. "The company moved -- changed its name. I don't know why I came here. It must have slipped my mind. We moved!"

"Jose is not here any longer. We let him go. He said you changed after that night."

"I – I don't—I don't talk to him -"

"He's afraid you'll say something. But I assured him you'd keep your stupid, bitching mouth shut." He slowly advanced on her now. The crowd around them didn't notice or care about the oddities in their exchange. "You seem like a responsible young lady. I wouldn't want you to run into a mighty catastrophe of your own making. I'm sure you know what's best."

"What's best?" Tessa stopped then. No matter how scared she thought she was, she wouldn't tolerate a threat. Melvin was no match for faith. Good over evil. Tessa stood for the good and wasn't about to back down.

"Yes," Melvin said. He stooped within two feet of her but wouldn't dare any closer. He could see her defiance and smell her will to fight. "Heaven forbid something should happen to you, some chance accident or fall that ends your life. It would be such a shame."

Without another word, Tessa turned from Melvin and marched back to the revolving doors without looking behind her until she was out of the light-tinted windowed lobby. Swiftly moving away from the entrance of the building, past the rushing crowd moving opposite her, fighting for their space on the line at the lobby's Coffeebucks. She stopped to look back into the glassed entry, being safe enough away then.

She did not find Melvin Rodriquez there.

He was gone again without a trace.